Julie, or Sylvia

This is one book from *The Ternion*, a series of novels published in 2024 under the #antiwrimo moniker. Please indulge in the others from the collection:

Escaping Emily

David Estringel, Alexandra Naughton, Risha Mae Ordas
ISBN-13: 979-8-9895422-3-9

Spark Bird

Jonathan Koven, Daniel DeRock, Julian Shendelman
ISBN-13: 979-8-9895422-5-3

Julie, or Sylvia

A Novel

Nicole Tallman
Ibrahim Sofiyullaha
Beryl Cooper

An #antiwrimo Book
Thirty West Publishing House

Julie, or Sylvia

ISBN-13: 979-8-9895422-4-6
Cover art by Jenn Zed
Jacket design by Josh Dale
Edited by Maryam Qureshi
Printed in the U.S.A.

For more titles and inquiries, please visit:
www.thirtywestph.com

The following chapters were penned by their respective authors.

Nicole Tallman: 1, 2, 5, 6, 9,10,13, 21, 21***, 27, 28, 29, 30, 31, 32, 33, 34, 39, 40, 41, 42, 43, 51, 52, 53, 54, 55, 60, 61, 62, 63, 65, 66, 67, 69, 73, 74, 76, 77, 78, 82, 83, 84, 85, 86, 87, and 88.

Ibrahim Sofiyullaha: 3, 4, 4.5, 7, 8, 14,15, 22, 23, 35, 36, 56, 57, 70, 71, 72, 79, 80, and 89.

Beryl Cooper: 4.5***, 11, 11***, 12, 15***,16, 17, 18, 19, 20, 24, 25, 26, 37, 38, 43***, 44, 45, 46, 47, 48, 49, 50, 58, 59, 64, 68, 72***, 75, 81, 88***, and 89***.

For Sylvia Plath

1.

The moment I placed my hands on the old oak board, I knew I was summoning my own death. My mother had told me not to speak to the spirits alone, but I'm bad at following rules and my mother is dead now anyway. How did she die? I still don't know.

Do you ever write letters you know no one will ever see or answer? I'm writing this one now—from the birch bed they have me strapped to. It's so dark in this room, and I'm scared and cold. It smells like dead chrysanthemums and snow.

I'm writing this letter with my mind. I have no pen or paper. Do you see my black words on the white wall? I write with ink, not blood. I'm not a monster. At least I don't think I am. My letter has no salutation, but it doesn't need one. You know you are dear. You know we'll all die. You know all there is to know. Just listen.

October is the month when the veil between the living and the dead is thinnest, and the spirits can use this fragility for their benefit. I am glass. They speak to me now. Their voices are violets, then dead leaves in the wind.

I say:

Explain magic.

They say:

A blizzard in summer.

I say:

Explain god.

They say:

A summer in snow.

I say:

Explain crucifixion.

They say:

A winter of nails.

I say:

Explain death.

They say:

A rose without thorns.

They add, unprompted:

A fall without doors.

It goes on like this for what feels like hours.

I must occupy my time here somehow, and my time is measured by seasons—not seconds or minutes, or hours, or days, or months, or years. These aren't seasons as you know them. There is no calendar or clock on the wall. But I know for certain it is spring in this room. I can feel it. I hear the frost breaking. And the purple crocuses are pushing through the snow.

Soon, there will be a trial. But I have no defense. Possession is not a defense for a devil, or a witch, or a madwoman. Which one am I? I no longer know what I am.

But I know there will be fire. I already feel the burn. And the rope. My wrists and ankles have gone numb.

I need you to know that I didn't kill my mother. She left a letter they say only I can see.

It says:

> *Dear Sylvia,*
>
> *The spirits are real, and so is the devil.*
>
> *Don't try to find me.*
>
> *I love you more than you know.*
>
> *Mom*

Have you see my mother's letter now?

Yesterday, a priest stopped by my bedside to pray. I couldn't bear the scent of him. Too clean, too pure. He thinks I'm either insane or possessed. There will be some kind of test. I know because I heard him talking to someone outside my door. I pretend to sleep when he enters my room. He thinks I don't understand Latin, but I do. He says this over and over again:

Deprecare Deum pacis, ut conterat satanam sub pedibus nostris, ne ultra valeat captivos tenere homines, et Ecclesiae nocere.[1]

The priest burns sage, frankincense, and myrrh in my room. He nails a cross above my bed. He crosses

---

[1] *Oh, pray to the God of peace that He may put Satan under our feet, so far conquered that he may no longer be able to hold men in captivity and harm the Church.*

himself. He contemplates a vial of holy water but doesn't douse me with it. I don't know his name, but he wants me to call him Father. If I could speak, I would. My own father is dead. It might be nice to call someone Father. But someone or something has taken my tongue.

2.

I'm starting to think I'm dead because no one nearby can hear what I say. Is everyone just ignoring me? I want to speak to my mother, but they've taken away my oak board. I wonder if I can build a new one. My mother said that birch drives out evil spirits. That must be why they've made me this special bed. They either think I'm evil or want to drive another evil away. Maybe it's a bit of both.

Until I have another board, I try talking to my mother with my mind.

I say:

Mother, can you hear me?

Mother says:

Yes, Love.

I say:

Am I dead?

Mother says:

No.

I say:

Where am I?

Mother says:

An asylum.

I say:

Tell me where you are.

Mother says:

I have to go.

I know she told me not to try to find her, but I need to know where she is. It's the not knowing that makes us crazy.

Some people say my mother was crazy. They say she killed herself but didn't leave a note. I don't believe this, and I hope you don't either because I've shown you her note. You can see it, and anything really, if you try hard enough.

A doctor enters my room and says he wants to ask me a series of questions. He unbinds my hands and hands me a clipboard. He asks me to write down the answers. I answer none of his questions. My hands are too numb to write. He should know this. I don't know his name. I'm sure he told me, but I wasn't listening. Let's just call him Dr. Dumb.

Dr. Dumb takes my blood pressure and my temperature. He listens to my heart. He says he wants to help me. I don't trust doctors. All they've ever done is hurt me and my mother with their poking and prodding, and their shocks and their drugs. I know they prefer me docile. They want to silence me and the voices. They don't like what I have to say, and they don't understand that the dead are my friends.

I prefer the dead to the living. The dead know what they've lost and don't waste time on triviality. I want to join them. I think that's probably why I'm here. I must have tried to join them again, but I don't remember.

I don't know why Dr. Dumb won't tell me exactly what I've done. Talking to the dead isn't a crime, but trying to kill oneself is. At least it is in this place I'm in. There's no mercy for the suffering.

I used to write poems with my friend Anne[2] before she died at her own hand. I've only ever wanted to be a famous writer. I've asked the spirits to help me in this regard. Sometimes, they take over my pen. It's not exactly automatic writing. It's not clear who is writing what. I'm not sure when I let them enter me that they ever leave. But the words flow better when they are around.

There is one spirit in particular who is extra creative. We wrote my last book together. Now he wants to write another. I'd tell you his name, but I don't want to share him. You must think I'm selfish. I only am when it comes to writing and food. I'm so hungry. They have me on a liquid diet. It's a terrible way to live. They've taken away all my pleasure. I can't eat. I can't write. I can't talk. I can't go for walks to clear my head. And where are my husband and children?

The doctors and priests here lock people up and mistreat them. How does anyone get better through deprivation? I don't think they want me to get better.

---

[2] Anne refers to the poetess Anne Sexton.

Maybe they put evil in me, so they have an excuse to kill me without punishment, without a tinge of remorse.

3.

The days in the asylum blurred into an endless nightmare, and the notion of time had become a distant, fading memory. Sylvia, or the entity that had taken control of her, remained trapped within the confines of her own mind. Dr. Dumb, as she had come to call him, continued his relentless prodding and probing, trying to unearth the truth, or perhaps break her spirit. The spirits remained her only solace.

In the lit room, the presence of spirits had grown stronger. Sylvia could feel them close, their whispered voices echoing in her mind. The creative spirit, the one she had written her last book with, was the most vocal. He urged her to continue their work, to bring their story to life. The desire to write, to escape into the world of words, was a lifeline in this cold, sterile place.

"Sylvia," he whispered, "the words, they are your salvation. Let them flow, let them set you free."

She closed her eyes and focused on the spirit's voice, allowing her mind to wander through the network of thoughts. The words poured forth like a torrent, and she wrote them down on the walls of her mind, where only she could see.

The spirits shared stories of their own, tales of lives

cut short and dreams unfulfilled. Sylvia felt a deep connection with them, for she, too, had known the pain of unfulfilled dreams. She couldn't help but wonder if her desire to be a famous writer had brought her to this precipice of madness, this border between life and death.

As the days turned into weeks, the room seemed to close in on her. The air grew heavier, and the darkness of the asylum became oppressive. Sylvia's hunger for both sustenance and words gnawed at her. She yearned for her husband and children, but they were nowhere to be found. Had they abandoned her, or had something sinister befallen them as well?

One day, during one of Dr. Dumb's questioning sessions, Sylvia decided to speak. She chose her words carefully, wanting to convey her desperation without revealing the full extent of her connection with the spirits. "Dr. Dumb, I need to know what has happened to my family. Where are they?"

The doctor studied her with a skeptical gaze, his eyes hidden behind round spectacles. "Your family, Sylvia? They are not here. You are alone, and you must focus on your own recovery."

Sylvia's heart sank. It was as if her family had been erased from existence. She couldn't accept that they had abandoned her, not without a word. She knew she had to find a way out, to uncover the truth that had been shrouded in darkness.

As the spirits continued to guide her thoughts, Sylvia began to piece together fragments of memories that had eluded her until now. The asylum, the mysterious circumstances of her confinement, the voices that whispered to her in the dead of night—they were all part of a puzzle she needed to solve.

One night, when the moon hung low in the sky and the spirits' presence was overwhelming, Sylvia decided. She would escape this room, this place of torment, and she would uncover the secrets that bound her here. With the help of the spirits, she would break free.

But freedom came at a price. The spirits demanded a pact, an agreement that would bind them to Sylvia even more closely. She hesitated, knowing that she was treading on dangerous ground, but the allure of escaping the asylum was too strong.

"I accept," she whispered into the darkness, sealing the pact with the spirits. It was a binding contract that would change the course of her existence, but Sylvia had little left to lose.

As the days turned into months, Sylvia's determination grew. She cultivated her connection with the spirits, learning to harness their power. With their guidance, she began to explore the asylum's secrets, discovering hidden passages and long-forgotten records.

The more she uncovered, the clearer it became that the asylum held its own dark history. It was a place of experimentation, of cruel treatments and secrets that were meant to remain buried. Sylvia was not the only one who had been tormented within these walls, and the spirits of the past cried out for justice.

But as Sylvia dug deeper into the asylum's mysteries, she also uncovered the truth about her own condition. It was a revelation that shook her to her core, leaving her questioning her own identity and the nature of the spirits that had become her companions.

4.

Sylvia's exploration of the asylum's secrets continued, and each discovery pushed her deeper into the maze of mysteries. With the spirits as her guides, she uncovered documents that hinted at unspeakable experiments performed on the patients, including the use of psychotropic substances and experimental treatments. It seemed the asylum had a dark history of attempting to harness the powers of the human mind, often with devastating consequences.

As she browsed further into the records, Sylvia began to suspect that the very same experiments that had driven her to the brink of madness were connected to the spirits she now communicated with. It was as if the asylum had become a nexus of supernatural energies, a place where the boundary between the living and the dead had grown thin, and where the spirits found a way to bridge the gap.

One evening, Sylvia uncovered a set of old diaries written by a former patient, a woman named Mary. Her writings described encounters with otherworldly beings and hinted at a connection to the spirits that now guided Sylvia. It was a chilling revelation, and Sylvia couldn't shake the feeling that Mary's story was intertwined with her own.

"I can hear them whispering in the darkness," Mary had written, "and their words, like black ink, flow through my veins. They promise me power and knowledge beyond the comprehension of mortals."

The spirits, too, had promised Sylvia knowledge and power. But what were their true intentions, and what price would she ultimately pay for her alliance with them?

Sylvia's pursuit of answers led her to a hidden chamber deep within the asylum. The room was adorned with strange symbols and sigils etched into the walls, an indication to the arcane rituals that had taken place there. In the center of the room, a heavy oak table held a collection of artifacts, including an ancient Ouija board.

The spirits stirred as Sylvia entered the chamber. "This is where it all began," they whispered. "This is where the barrier between the worlds was breached."

Sylvia approached the Ouija board with a mixture of curiosity and dread. It was a conduit, a bridge to the other side, and she could feel the spirits' anticipation. They urged her to use it, to contact the entity that had once been Mary.

When her fingers touched the planchette, the room grew colder, and a gust of wind swept through the chamber. The planchette began to move on its own, spelling out words with an eerie grace.

"Who are you?" Sylvia asked.

The planchette responded, "I am Mary, and I am not alone."

Sylvia's heart raced. "What do you want from me, Mary?"

Mary's response sent shivers down Sylvia's spine. "To break the cycle, to set us free. The asylum is a prison, not just for the living, but for the spirits that have become trapped within its walls. You can help us, Sylvia."

The spirits that had been Sylvia's constant companions echoed Mary's plea. They urged her to help them find a way to release the souls trapped in the asylum, to close the rift between the living and the dead.

But as Sylvia dug deeper into the task at hand, she realized that the answers were not so easily obtained. The rituals required were dangerous, and the risks were high. The spirits demanded sacrifices, and Sylvia had to weigh the cost of her actions against the possibility of setting them all free.

4.5

In the weeks that followed, Sylvia, Mary, and the spirits began their quest to break the cycle of suffering that had plagued the asylum for generations. Together, they performed ancient rites and rituals, seeking to mend the tears in the fabric of reality.

But as their efforts intensified, so did the opposition. Dr. Dumb and the other staff members of the asylum grew increasingly suspicious of Sylvia's activities. They had no intention of allowing her to uncover the truth, to bring light to the darkness that had shrouded their actions for so long.

✳ ✳ ✳

The text cut off there. It was handwritten, and the perspective jumped, and it wasn't entirely clear as to where or when the events described took place. It also wasn't clear how old the text itself was, or who wrote it, or why.

I found it lodged in a crushed wall on a demo job. We're not supposed to keep things, but I tucked it into my bag and read it on the bus home. Then I forgot about it for several years. My life is horrifying enough without any specters, without the ramblings of a tongueless maybe-murderess. Capitalism, you know, is horror enough. When I want to be scared I read statistics about health care and sea level rise.

So why am I thinking of that strange fragment again? I'll get there. I realize that first I want to do a bit of a preface, or technical note, so if anyone comes across this text and finds it similarly disjointed and cut-off, they'll at least understand what they're looking at and have a sense of why the text is in its form. And that possibility of a future-understanding, even if not my own, is maybe the one thing to drive and comfort me now.

I'm being dramatic, but it's earned. Trust me.

Ok so I'm dictating this text as a record of my thoughts and observations. And I'm thinking of the fragment I found because lately I've been walking past the site where I found it, again and again, drawn by the seep there.

The spot's ordinary; a parklet, a strip mall. Decent pizza.

Maybe two weeks ago I walked by and saw the seep. I didn't know what it was then. I don't know now either. What I saw was a little dark liquid pool. Blood, obviously, and fresh. I called the police, but no victims were apparent, and they knew nothing of the blood's source. Some of the shopkeepers asked and were told they could clean it up; the spot was not an active crime scene. So, I watched, and they scrubbed off the asphalt, and I walked on.

The next day I returned to ask the shop clerks whether anyone knew what caused the blood pool. But as I approached the shopping plaza I saw the blood was back, and it was covering the original spot as well as a few other small patches. I walked into the pizza shop and the employees hadn't seen anything violent. They sent a guy to clean the asphalt, and said they'd ask the manager to put up an extra security camera.

I came back again the day after. The blood was back. Maybe thicker slightly? Maybe there was an extra patch or two? I watched the pizza clerk clean the spots again. Each revealed little cracks in the pavement when cleaned. I worked a napkin into one and fished it out bloody. Clots and strands, the brighter liquid. Each fissure yielded similar results.

I kept returning. The pizza man told me he was cleaning every few hours now, had started a rotation with the cashiers at the smoke shop and the water filtration place. No one wanted the health department to get involved.

That's when I should have stopped. But I am bored and underemployed, and I could not pass up investigating a stigmatic parking lot. So, I returned. I cataloged the leaks, measured the seeping crevices, blood volumes and densities, and the rate of new blood spots appearing.

Then maybe five days ago I began to hear the sounds, gurgling and wet but not the flow of underground blood. No these were uncanny almost-throat sounds, vocal. It was then that I remembered the text, that stolen demolition artifact. It was then that I read it again. It was then that I should have quit.

But I returned to the site with microphones. By now the plaza was taped off and someone had placed an 'under construction' sign at the parking lot entrance. I ducked the tape and began taping. At night I'd listen back, filter out frequencies, try different playback speeds, try playing backwards. The sound was just on the border or being voice, just at the threshold of sense.

And then yesterday I swore I made out a threat in the hiss, or a warning maybe, though I couldn't tell you the words. I mean I perceived a message in that sound that was beyond or may before language, something irreducible. This thrilled me; I had never felt a communion with anything..

So, I returned to the lot, which was now a kind of asphalt blood swamp. A pair of coyotes lapped at the edge. I imagined it grown thick with reeds, lilies floating, blood koi drifting and shimmering. The sound, or sounds, had grown louder too. I couldn't tell if it was a single modulating sound or a mix of different almost-voices. Is a chorus a singular noun? I mean yes, but...

I reached into the blood. It was just a few inches to the bottom, not even enough to wet my wrist. I felt along until I reached a seeping crevice. I could feel the subtle outflow, warmer and denser, and I plunged my fingers into the opening. The ground was firm but gave way as I pried. Slowly, I widened it enough to slip my fingers in, then my arm to the elbow. Down there the blood was almost hot, and I could feel solid bits floating by—grit and viscera? I don't really know what it was. I retracted and cleaned my arm.

The sound was entering me. I mean it was more or other than hearing, a passing-through. I must be precise here. There was no instruction. There was no auditory hallucination of a pronouncement. But from the fact of the sound came the image of a raft, and other more obscure images that I cannot or do not wish to describe.

I reached back into the widened blood-mouth and trawled with my fingers for a solid bit to examine. What I caught first had the shape and trail of a dislodged eye. At that point I thought again of the text I found in that same spot. Oblique and tongueless voices, death and pharmaceuticals. Madness. I released the maybe-eye and withdrew my arm, then hurried back to my apartment.

There I dug out that found text. I knew I would not stop returning to the sound and seep. I needed to understand it. I need to, I mean, in the present. I cannot just ignore a growing blood swamp, and besides the alternative is precarity and temp jobs and Mitch downstairs offering craft beer and ethically questionable anecdotes. I also know that one should be wary of aural communion with quasi-telepathic primordial vibrations coming from a blood lake. So, I am documenting. I read the found text into the record, and I am explaining or at least narrating my actions. It is unlikely to do me much good, but it's something—a trace at least if I am later unable to explain things.

I'm going to sleep for a bit, and in the morning I'll return to the site. I have rope and good boots and some excavation tools. I want to get closer to the blood source, to the sound home. I have the sense, perhaps wrong, that those things are one, and that it exists. I am not so naive to believe in answers, but still. The sound is real, and the swamp, and I will go as far as I can.

5.

Mary is my only real friend here. I realize that my husband and children are not coming to visit, and I have not been able to reach my mother again. I know she said she had to go, but I didn't believe she would break our ability to connect. I've tried reaching her with my mind and the board when I manage to unbind myself and wander in the darkness of the night.

I am one of many patients here, and I've found there is a golden hour when no one checks on me, and I am free to explore. If I am good, surely I will earn the right to be unbound during the day and perhaps explore the grounds outside. I must prove to them who I am. They don't seem to believe me. There is a driver's license in my purse. If only I could find it! What have they done with my belongings? I couldn't have arrived here completely empty handed.

I suppose it doesn't matter. I have fingerprints, saliva, and blood. They can trace my identity. I am in the system, like every good American. Oh, but I'm British now! Why won't they admit who I am? It's as if they don't want anyone to know I'm alive. Am I more interesting dead?

I suppose death is when people pay more attention.

I wonder if my books are selling better now that people think I'm dead. That is what they think, right? That's what Dr. Dumb told me. Maybe people will care more about my poetry now. Or maybe I should write another novel. I know my first was too dark for some. People shudder at talk of suicide, but it must have sold at least a few copies by now. Well, I'm going to focus on my poems. There is no stopping it. I don't have the distractions I had before. No one is crying for me to cook, or launder, or to deal with them in any way, and I can focus on what I was truly meant to do.

Don't get me wrong. I love my children, but they don't understand my need to write. They are far too small! And my husband? He only wants to write and drink and sleep around. I shouldn't speak of him this way. I could get sued for slander or libel. Am I speaking or writing? I can't tell anymore. I still don't understand what has happened to my tongue. I simply can't feel it. I really think they've cut it out, but maybe it's all the drugs Dr. Dumb has given me. They make me so disoriented and numb. And yesterday, more shocks to the head. Jesus, they want me dead. I just know it.

I wrote a poem on the wall last night. Surely you can see it and recognize that it's me.

Holy Mary

They've cut out my tongue!
They don't want me to speak!
These doctors and priests
With their dumb potions and waters—
Nothing here is holy.
They would kill me if they could.

I lie here so small, so thin.
Don't believe them!
Small men with their poison pens,
Mary is my only friend.
She is the one solid thing I lean on
During these black, bleak times.

Do you see the devil?
It's not me! It's Wevill! [3]
It's Ted! [4] He shows himself in red
And the dead, and the snow.
His heart is so dead and cold, he burns
The room with frost from his fallen angels. [5]
Oh, I have also invented a new form! It's called "The Devil's
Form." It's three stanzas of 6 lines each. "The 666," I also
call it. Ha! They'll really think I'm possessed now.

---

[3] Wevill refers to Assia Wevill, Sylvia Plath's husband's mistress.
[4] Ted refers to Sylvia Plath's husband Ted Hughes, who was
having an affair with Assia Wevill.
[5] To read a decent "Mary" poem, refer to Sylvia Plath's poem
"Mary's Song" in her book, *Ariel.*

Mary says I should keep writing my new book on the wall and Pan[6] says so, too. Oh, hell! I've disclosed my ghostwriter's name. Now he's going to want credit. Well, celebrities do this all the time: Take credit for books others have written. I'm a bit of a celebrity myself now. I just know it. Death has boosted me to the fame I always wanted. Too bad I wasn't able to bask in the spotlight while I was alive and out and about in the world.

Maybe they'll even award me a posthumous Pulitzer. Wouldn't that be the bee's knees? A real kick in the head, or whatever it is they say these days. I've lost track of time, but now it is winter again. I know because the snow has come down in mounds and the elms have a different scent to them. I can smell it from here. It's as if they have been raped raw by the winter wind and bitter cold.

I think there may only be two seasons here because I haven't seen summer or fall. What a special kind of hell. It would be nice to have a little relief from the cold. I seem to always have a head cold now too. It's a form of torture.

I can't stop thinking that maybe Ted put me here. I know he wanted to get rid of me. But would he lock me up? Keep me away from my children? What would he tell them when they ask for me?

---

[6] To read two of Sylvia Plath's most notable Ouija board-inspired poems, refer to "Ouija" and "Dialogue Over a Ouija Board."

6.

Father is back to pay me another visit. I don't think he likes my new poem much. He is pacing the room and has brought reinforcements—another priest he calls Gabriel. Gabriel looks so scared and weak to me. Like a mouse being chased by an owl. They recite the same prayer over and over to drive away the devil, and they are dousing me now in their "holy" water. It smells like peroxide or salt. Maybe it's made of water from the ocean? Well, it doesn't burn me at all. Surely this must prove I am not possessed.

The priests want me to respond, but they never call me by my proper name. I find it disrespectful. Just to hear them say *Sylvia* would give me hope that I haven't lost everything. What am I without my identity? Without all that I have worked for.

I've done so much in 30 years. More than some do in a whole lifetime. Why, I have forever altered the confessional canon! And for the better, I must say.

Some might say I am the best poet of the 20th century! And not just the best woman poet. You know how some men like to remind women that we surely couldn't be better at something than they are. Well, I know I am better in this regard, and so was Anne.

She, like my mother, is another I can't seem to reach anymore. Why has Anne cut me off in this way? I can't get an answer. I even tried to send her my new poem, but she didn't respond. Maybe she doesn't like it? It's probably not my best work. I'm so medicated that it's hard to write. I also don't have my books or my typewriter. A writer needs her trusty tools. And something to eat besides this dreadful broth they are feeding me. I am wasting away to nothing but bone. Who will recognize this skeleton I've become?

Dr. Horder![7] Where is Dr. Horder? Why hasn't he come to see me, or sent the nurse he said he would? I'm starting to worry even more now about the children. I know the doctors want me to focus on myself, but who is caring for my babies? Ted and that Weavy Asshole? Oh, I am just sick at the thought of it! I must get out of here. Good behavior will surely get me released. I can be a good girl. The best girl even! Perhaps I should stop focusing on writing and communing with the spirits and simply plot my escape.

Mary can come with me. I want to save the others but am not sure I have the energy. So many have suffered here! How can I bear all this weight in my weakened state? How can I possibly free me, along with all these trapped, tortured souls?

---

[7] Dr. Horder refers to Dr. John Horder, Sylvia Plath's physician.

7.

Sylvia's connection to the spirits, particularly Mary, had grown stronger, their collective efforts now focused on a daring escape plan.

Sylvia, despite her weakened state, was determined to break free from the confines of the asylum. The days were long, filled with the echoes of her own thoughts and the distant, fearful whispers of the other patients. She couldn't forget her children, her husband, or the life she once knew, but the asylum had become a twisted purgatory where time itself seemed to have lost its meaning.

One evening, during the golden hour when the staff's vigilance waned, Sylvia took her first tentative steps toward freedom. With Mary as her silent accomplice, she managed to pick the lock on her restraints and quietly made her way down the dimly lit hallway.

The asylum was a labyrinth of secrets, a place where the sins of the past were concealed behind every door. Sylvia had glimpsed the suffering of other patients, their haunted eyes and hushed voices revealing the horrors they had endured. Their silent pleas for help filled her with a sense of responsibility.

Sylvia's escape plan was risky, but it was also the only chance for her and the others to reclaim their lives. As she navigated the maze-like layout of the facility, she uncovered hidden passageways and locked doors, each concealing a piece of the asylum's dark history.

Dr. Dumb and the other staff members remained vigilant, their suspicions growing with each passing day. They sensed that Sylvia was no longer the docile patient they had once known. She had become a woman with a mission, driven by a determination that could not be quelled.

But Sylvia was not alone in her quest for freedom. The spirits, with their spectral wisdom and ethereal presence, guided her every move. They whispered warnings of danger, provided insight into the asylum's layout, and served as her silent companions on this treacherous journey.

As Sylvia ventured deeper into the asylum, she encountered patients who had been confined for years, their minds fractured by the inhumane treatments they had endured. She knew that their salvation, their chance at a second life, rested on her shoulders. The weight of their suffering fueled her resolve.

The night was Sylvia's ally, providing cover for her clandestine operations. The asylum, shrouded in darkness, seemed to echo with the voices of the past, the anguished cries of those who had suffered within its walls.

The spirits whispered a mantra of hope as Sylvia continued her journey: "Break the cycle, set us free."

It was a plea that resonated not only with the spirits but also with the other patients who longed for release from their torment. Sylvia's path to freedom had become a mission of salvation, a quest to unshackle the lost souls of the asylum.

But the darkness held its secrets close, and Sylvia's escape was fraught with peril. The staff grew increasingly suspicious, and the spirits warned of impending danger. The asylum had become a battleground, where the forces of light and darkness clashed in a desperate bid for supremacy.

As Sylvia stood at the threshold of escape, she knew that the final battle was yet to come. The asylum's past, its horrors and its secrets, would be revealed. The spirits and the souls of the patients cried out for justice, and Sylvia was their beacon of hope.

With determination and the spirits as her guides, Sylvia prepared for the reckoning that lay ahead. The asylum's walls, once an impenetrable fortress, would bear witness to the resilience of the human spirit and the unyielding power of the supernatural.

8.

Sylvia's memories of her family were a bittersweet tapestry woven with love and despair. In the quiet corners of her mind, she could still hear the laughter of her children and feel the warmth of her husband's embrace. But those moments of happiness were overshadowed by the relentless storm that had raged within the Plath household.

Her husband, Ted, was a complex figure. Handsome and charismatic, he possessed a magnetic charm that drew people to him. But beneath the veneer of his charm lay a darkness, a riotous sea of emotions that Sylvia had struggled to navigate.

Their marriage had been a tempestuous affair, marked by passion and pain. Ted's infidelity had cast a long shadow over their relationship, leaving Sylvia torn between her love for him and the agony of betrayal. The scars of their tumultuous union had left her wounded, her heart bleeding with each new wound.

The children, Frieda and Nicholas, had been caught in the crossfire of their parents' disruptive love. Sylvia's love for her children was unwavering, but the demands of her burgeoning career had often left her torn between motherhood and her pursuit of literary success.

Frieda, the elder of the two, had inherited her mother's fiery spirit and creative flair. Her boundless energy and fierce independence had been both a source of pride and a challenge for Sylvia. She saw in Frieda a reflection of herself, a young woman destined for greatness but burdened by the weight of expectation.

Nicholas, the younger sibling, had been the family's gentle soul. His innocence had been a balm to Sylvia's troubled heart, a reminder of the purity of a child's love. But the tumultuous nature of their family had left its mark on Nicholas as well, and his young heart had been burdened by the strife that surrounded him.

The Plath family had been a world of contradictions, a place where love and torment existed in a delicate balance. Sylvia's desire to provide a stable, loving home for her children had often been at odds with the chaos that raged within her own heart.

As Sylvia's journey within the asylum continued, her thoughts often turned to her family. She yearned to be reunited with her children, to hold them in her arms and tell them how much she loved them. The thought of their absence haunted her, and the guilt of being separated from them weighed heavily on her soul.

In the asylum's darkest moments, when the spirits whispered their warnings and the staff's suspicions grew, Sylvia found solace in the memories of her family. She clung to the images of her children's smiles, the warmth of their laughter, and the love that had once filled their home.

The path to freedom was a treacherous one, and Sylvia knew that the asylum's secrets were a network that she would have to navigate. But the promise of reuniting with her family, of finding the happiness that had so often eluded her, was a beacon of hope that guided her through the darkness.

As she ventured deeper into the asylum's mysteries, Sylvia was driven by the need to break free, not only for her sake but for the sake of her children. The Plath family's story was one of love and pain, of hopes and shattered dreams, and Sylvia was determined to ensure that its legacy would be one of resilience and redemption.

The family she had left behind remained at the forefront of her mind, a reminder of the love that had once bound them together. As Sylvia continued her journey, she held onto the hope that she would one day be reunited with Frieda and Nicholas, and that their family's story would find its long-awaited resolution.

9.

The nurses wake me and tell me there is someone here to see me. I figure it may be Father or Gabriel, but in walks a person I haven't seen before—a woman. She says she is an English professor from Oxford, and she wants to see my poems. I'm just so happy someone besides the doctors, nurses, priests, and Mary can see me. This means I'm not dead after all!

The nurse unbinds me and hands me a clipboard with paper so I can communicate with the professor since I still cannot speak. I wonder if perhaps they can fashion me a prosthetic tongue. Fortunately, the nurses here are smarter than "the doctors.

I tell the professor via clipboard that my newest poem is on the wall. She says she cannot see it. I don't understand what is wrong with her and everyone else. The writing is literally on the wall! But I suppose there's nothing I can do about this predicament. I will write "Holy Mary" on the clipboard for her. My poetry is one of the few ways I can convince people of who I am, at least I hope I can. I simply can't bear to be here much longer. Oh now, don't think I'm being dramatic. My moods are all over the place. Dr. Dumb and the nurses have loosened my restraints, so my wrists aren't as numb. I really can't manage, but I have to pretend I'm ok if I ever want to see the light of day.

I write the poem by hand and hand the clipboard to the professor. She reads it slowly, more than once. I trace her eyes as they move across the paper. Her face does not register any reaction. She asks me if I have more. I tell her I am writing a whole book of them on the wall. She tells me the poems must be on paper because she can't read them on the wall. I tell her I need a typewriter, paper, ribbon, pens, and a few books and magazines if I'm going to produce my best work. She asks me if I can use a laptop instead. I tell her I don't know what that is. She looks surprised but says she will get me the supplies I requested.

The professor asks me which books I need. I ask for my thesaurus, a regular dictionary, and a rhyming one. I tell her I also want to read the new books by the American poets I'm into, especially Lowell, Merwin, Rich, Sexton, Snodgrass, and Starbuck. And for old time's sake, Auden, Eliot, and Yeats. I ask her not to send me any books by modern British poets, and especially not Ted's. I also ask for *The New Yorker*. She writes this all down on a piece of paper from the clipboard and says she will come back soon to visit me again.

This is the best I've felt since I've been here. I am starting to see a way out that may not involve a sneaky escape. And if I can write good poems, I can start sending my work out again! People will want to read and see me. They will buy my new book. It will be even more successful than the last one, I just know it! Ted will be so jealous. Oh, he'll be sorry he left me for that evil woman!

10.

I have another visitor. This time it's Pan, and he arrives unannounced. He's starting to startle me. He knocks on the walls of my head and says I'm not writing quickly enough. It's gotten to the point that I no longer need a Ouija board to summon him. He just appears at will and tells me what to write, and the words come so fast that I often can't catch them fast enough.

I tell him the professor needs the poems on paper, so he needs to slow down. He says he doesn't trust this professor. He asks who she is and what her credentials are for evaluating my work. I tell him she didn't tell me her name or give me her card. He says I must ask the next time she comes to see me. In the meantime, Pan says we need to write another 6-6-6 poem. He wants me to write about the bees buzzing in hell. Haven't I written enough about bees?[8] He tells me it's what my father would want.[9] He knows how to push my buttons. Pan also never wearing clothes. He wants to seduce me.

---

[8] For an extraordinary set of Sylvia Plath bee poems, refer to the bee sequence ("The Bee Meeting," "The Arrival of the Bee Box," "Stings," "The Swarm," and "Wintering") in *Ariel.*
[9] Sylvia Plath's father, Dr. Otto Plath, was a respected entomologist, with a specific expertise on bumblebees, and the author of the 1934 book, *Bumblebees and Their Ways.*

I tell Pan my father is dead and what he wants doesn't matter. Pan says I need to write the bee poem. It's what the people want, too. The poets want the moon, but the people want the bees—all their honey and sting.

I tell him that Father and Gabriel do not like the devil's form. Pan says he doesn't trust the priests either, or that's why he always disappears whenever the two of them are around. He says Dr. Dumb is just as bad. He tells me there is nothing wrong with me. That no one but him can recognize my genius. He also says Mary is sweet, but not to let her distract me from my goal. I am here to write, not to save souls. Pan says souls are what the priests need to focus on. He also asks me if I think priests are actually good people. I tell him I don't know. What is good anyway?

I tell Pan that now he is distracting me from writing. He says he wants us to write this bee poem together. I think the theme he's suggesting is kind of dumb, along with his words, but I go along with his clumsy verse because I'm too tired to write my own today.

Killer Bees

The halls of hell
Are combs of killer bees.
They've drunk all the honey,
There's none left for me.
The drunken bees swarm my dumb
Head, their yellow hearts full of sting.

I've been swallowed now
Without taste or tongue.
I feel the swell of hell in this
Black, black room without church
Or bell, just doctors and priests
Who want me to prove I'm the one.

Silver tongued, I'm the sharpest tool,
Sylvia, the girl who trees and roots
For me, whose soul is bleeding red
Whose heart is dead with dread—
I know that only you and Pan
Can save this grave of words I've left.

11.

Meanwhile, across the street from the hospital, a slim white man types a memo. This is the really scary part—that the memo supplants material truth with state-recognized fact; that the cruel, dull man can wield that kind of magic. This is called bureaucracy, a kind of slant rhyme for necromancy. But not really the stuff of horror books. So, to suit the genre, his body splits in two, lengthwise crown to genitals, spine as a hinge, with great razor teeth gnashing in the gap, and this awful mouth-body whirls through the office building consuming.

Other suited office men split similarly and whirl about, tearing through walls and colleagues alike.

This goes on for some time, a day or three, and the city shuts down. The asylum doctors and attendants, those that survive, stop coming into work. The one who calls herself Sylvia wanders out into the street. A mouth-body in Armani whirls past and eviscerates a child. Sylvia's stippled with splatter. She licks a drop from the tip of her nose.

Sylvia makes her way to the riverbank, thinks the better of it, breaks into an abandoned gas station and loads a bag with salted nuts, sour gummies, beef jerky.

Finding it private, she shits behind the checkout counter then empties the cash register in case money might still be useful. She walks on with her snack bag slung over her shoulder and a two liter of Cherry Coke. Her stride is powerful, untroubled, and in the sun at that moment she is stunning.

Next she loots a hardware store, grabs several cans of spray paint and a large hammer. The hammer is for protection, though the mouth-bodies all assiduously avoid her. Well, they let her be at least, though they do seem to orbit her, to devour anyone who comes too close. In the hours since her freedom, Sylvia's seen a pair of elderly women reduced to ribbons, and the child, and a handful of joggers. A strapping constable was chewed down to a mustache and a pool of blood.

Coyotes lope from the canyons to dine on the viscera.

Sylvia scratches one vigorously between the ears as it laps cop blood at the edge of a strip mall parking lot. She calls it Mother and they travel together through the mostly abandoned city. A month passes. Sylvia and Mother live off canned goods and session beers. Sylvia spray-paints overwrought verse across a wide range of retailers and apartments. It isn't good. That is, poetry-as-vandalism is surely good in the abstract, but Sylvia's work is obvious and clunky. It doesn't bear copying down.

I'm back again. Couldn't record in the blood lake; I don't have the right equipment for underwater dictation. So, I'll try to catch you up on what happened.

As I promised, I returned to the sound, the almost-voices, the seep. It was tentacling out into the street and the fast cars sprayed blood like puddle water. I pictured the stunned drivers arriving home to crimson undercarriages, what they must imagine.

I knew wading about in the morass was insufficient, so I inflated a small rubber boat and pulled on a scuba suit. Then I paddled to the center of the thick pond, donned the breathing apparatus, and dove in. Although I wore a headlamp, I could barely see more than a few inches from my face. Even then all I made out were bobbing fragments and shadows. So, I groped my way to a crevice where I could feel the fresh, hot flow, and I pried that open until I could slip inside to the under-layer, then I swam in that channel, which I now take to be a kind of artery, perhaps, until I reached an unexpected beach.

I pulled myself ashore and removed the breathing apparatus. The beach consisted of tiny, sharp rocks, or so it felt. There was no light besides my headlamp, and I was afraid that if I trained it on the ground I would discover that this was a beach of teeth. I walked a few meters. The ground leveled and firmed. My lamp shone on nothing. I continued.

The sound was louder here, and the images it passed through by head and body were sharper, and for that reason more disturbing. I don't think I would describe all of them even if I could, for fear of what you might think of me for having held them. A sampling: a half-manatee cauterized at the cut; a breast with blind occluded cat eyes; a steamboat feeling depressed during Rush Week. Those are the ones I can most closely pin down. The others I perceived with absolute clarity but cannot begin to fix with language.

I walked on for an indeterminable period of time. That communion, the almost-voices becoming asymptotically closer to voices...

Then I saw a sign, wooden and painted with large block letters. APOLOGIES. A small black arrow pointed to a little shelf below on which sat a manila envelope. *Second Installment* was written by hand on the front. I opened it, of course, to find a continuation of the odd, disjointed text I'd discovered in the walls of that demolished building years ago. The Sylvia Story. I read the enclosed chapters by lamplight. This felt wrong. More wrong even than the blood seep, the underworld beneath it, or even the sound-image-communion that had drawn me here. And the echoes in the text—I couldn't go there.

Still, I couldn't leave it either. I tucked the manuscript into a drybag and made my way back to the artery. It would be nearly impossible to retrace my path to the surface through the black and wet, but I left a digital beacon at the breach point. The crevice was already self-suturing when I arrived, so I had to re-pry it open enough to squeeze out. I headed home and began this recording.

Tomorrow I will return with gear for a proper expedition.

12.

Sylvia and Mother curl together in a king-sized bed in the middle of an abandoned Ikea. Several of her former asylum-mates have taken up residency in the store as well, and the assorted madfolk share regular meatball dinners and take turns assembling bookshelves and end tables just as they once sat doing jigsaw puzzles in the common rooms.

A pack of the mouth-bodies also moved in, but they do not harm the madfolk. They all wear high-end tailored suits and when they swing closed can be found with espressos and thoughts on derivative swaps. But if anyone sane approaches the Ikea, they uniformly unhinge and characteristically whirl, and they razor and consume. Thus, over a few weeks, the Ikea perimeter is encircled with a dark bloodstain and swarms of vultures take to standing sentry on the building's bright blue roof.

Mother brings to bed the occasional ear or femur.

Sylvia takes up haiku.

The poetry of / Scandinavian design / is in the umlaut

Mother coyote / bit the lips off of my crush / so I could kiss them

Sylvia believes, at the moment, in poetics as truth-telling and arranges the lips seductively on her pillow.

Her crush, mad also (prone to hallucinations that the city is built on the back of an enormous sleeping woman), scabs over in the makeshift recovery ward that the mouth-bodies set up in the Kitchen Design Center.

This is an idyll. Sylvia stretches and is happy and no memories intrude to sweep away the sweetness. Such states cannot last.

13.

This new world is so disorienting. Why am I living at IKEA? I'm much more of a Selfridges girl.

I've drunk enough lingonberry juice here to last a lifetime. One can only take so many trips to the buffet, and I'm completely froyo-ed out.

The spirits have stopped talking to me, so I must face real life alone with Mother, the madfolk, and mouth-bodies. I don't have the asylum drugs or electric shocks to sedate me. I am awake all the time. My nerves are frayed and my mind spins and spins like a carousel, or one of those tiny ballerinas trapped in the music box of her mind. Controlled pain is better than the alternative. I'm starting to miss Dr. Dumb and the nurses who would check on me periodically.

I search for clues in the ceiling panels. The words are written in the blood of all who have passed. The fluorescent lights scream, YOU'RE NEXT, SYLVIA!!!!!! I know my end is near.

The sun is as depressed as I am, and no longer wants to come out. The moon is tired of shining all the time. (She used to switch shifts with the sun.) So, the moon goes on strike and now there is only the faint light of stars outside. They too will likely soon strike, although there is no union for celestial rights.

I would like Father and Gabriel to exorcise my suffering, but they are nowhere to be found. And the professor who promised to return with my books and supplies surely won't come find me here at IKEA. She looks like the type who only shops at Harrods.

I'd like nothing more than a glass of sherry, a roasted chicken, and a hot bath. I hope for my children's sake that they aren't alive to see this. This new world is no place for the innocent to live.

I think about how I'll never sun or moon bathe again. And all the trees are dead now too. I will write an elegy for the elms.[10] Come to think of it, there's hardly anything left that requires oxygen to breathe. How am I still here? And Mother? How can I be sure we're alive?

---

[10] To read a good poem about elms, refer to Sylvia Plath's "Elm," also in *Ariel*. At this point, if you don't own a copy of *Ariel*, you may just want to buy the book. It will make these footnotes, and the book as a whole, much more meaningful.

14.

Dr. Dumb watched Sylvia from the shadows, his eyes fixated on her as she sat in the makeshift living room of the abandoned Ikea. The professor had successfully brought her the requested writing supplies, and Sylvia was now fervently scribbling poems, her haunted eyes darting across the pages. She was a woman possessed, or at least, that's what it seemed. But what if there was more to it than met the eye?

The professor had noticed it too. The sudden transformation from a woman who believed herself to be Sylvia Plath to a focused, driven poet was perplexing. Was it merely a symptom of her mental illness, or was there something else at play? Sylvia's work was far from coherent, but there was a raw energy to it that couldn't be ignored. The professor couldn't help but wonder: Was it possible that Sylvia Plath's spirit had somehow inhabited this woman, guiding her hand in creating these poems?

Dr. Dumb had his own suspicions. He had seen countless patients, but there was something about Sylvia that gnawed at him. The way she wrote, the intensity in her eyes—it was as if she was on the verge of discovering some profound truth. And it terrified him. What if she unveiled something that the world wasn't ready to accept? Was her newfound creativity a product of her madness, or was it a glimpse into a hidden brilliance?

As Sylvia continued to write, her mind a whirlwind of words and images, Dr. Dumb contemplated his next move. He needed to uncover the truth behind this enigma. He couldn't allow Sylvia to escape and potentially reveal whatever secrets lay within her. But the professor was watching, too, and she seemed equally determined to understand the mystery.

She banged hard on the gadget made available to her, scribing cryptic, mind-boggling verses that only she seems to have a clue of what they meant, or, as her faceless face suggests, not even her, maybe no one. She poured:

In the turf of madness, a soul lost at sea,
Whispers of a life once lived, can it truly be?
Eyes that peer into the void, searching for a face,
Within the shadows of the mind, a haunting, empty space.

A river of forgotten dreams, its waters dark and deep,
In the wreckage of the past, secrets buried, secrets keep,
Sylvia, who am I, an enigma unconfined,
In this endless maze of questions, truth I long to find.

Meanwhile, Sylvia's quest for escape persisted. She had befriended the other madfolk in the Ikea, forming an odd but strangely functional community. The mouth-bodies, the guardians of this peculiar haven, allowed them to coexist, as long as no outsiders approached. But Sylvia couldn't stay hidden forever. Her true identity, or the identity she believed to be true, beckoned her.

The questions weighed heavily on everyone involved. Who was Sylvia, really? Was she just a delusional woman, or was she a vessel for a legendary poet's spirit? The tension was palpable as Dr. Dumb, the professor, and Sylvia herself danced around these unspoken inquiries. They were on the cusp of a revelation, and it was only a matter of time before the truth would reveal itself.

15.

The tension in the abandoned Ikea was palpable. Dr. Dumb, the enigmatic professor, and the madfolk watched as Sylvia feverishly wrote, her pen slashing through the pages like a possessed artist. The room was filled with an almost oppressive energy, a sense that something significant was about to unfold.

Sylvia's poems were growing increasingly disjointed and surreal. Her words painted vivid and disturbing images of a world only she could comprehend. It was as if her mind had become a portal to a dimension of madness and creativity, and she was the conduit through which it flowed.

As she wrote, her eyes were wide and unblinking, her gaze fixed on a point only she could see. The professor observed her with a mixture of fascination and trepidation. It was as though Sylvia had tapped into some otherworldly source of inspiration, and the professor couldn't help but wonder if this was the moment when the truth would reveal itself.

Dr. Dumb, too, felt a growing unease. He had seen many patients in his career, but Sylvia was unlike any of them. Her transformation from a delusional woman who believed she was Sylvia Plath to a creative force of nature was bewildering. He needed to understand what had triggered this change, and if there was any way to harness it.

Sylvia's hands trembled as she continued to write. The words spilled onto the paper; each line more enigmatic than the last. Her fingers moved with a desperation that bordered on madness. She was a woman possessed, or so it seemed.

But the truth was far more disturbing.

As the minutes ticked by, the tension in the room grew almost unbearable. The madfolk watched Sylvia in awe, their faces a mix of confusion and wonder. They had become accustomed to her eccentric behavior, but this was something else entirely.

And then, it happened.

Sylvia's hand suddenly stopped. She dropped the pen, her face contorting in pain. The room fell into an eerie silence, broken only by her labored breathing. The professor and Dr. Dumb rushed to her side, concern etched on their faces.

"What's happening to her?" the professor exclaimed, her voice trembling.

Dr. Dumb examined Sylvia, trying to make sense of her distress. It was as if some unseen force had taken hold of her, and now it was releasing its grip. He could feel her pulse racing beneath his fingers.

Sylvia's eyes, once wide and unblinking, now began to focus. She looked up at the concerned faces hovering over her and took a deep, shuddering breath.

"Julie," she whispered, her voice barely audible.

The room seemed to freeze as the word hung in the air. Julie? Who was Julie? The madfolk exchanged bewildered glances, and the professor and Dr. Dumb stared at Sylvia, searching for answers.

And then, with a startling clarity, Sylvia spoke again, her voice stronger this time.

"My name is Julie," she declared, her eyes locking onto Dr. Dumb's. "I am not Sylvia Plath."

The revelation hung in the air, a heavy truth that no one was prepared for. The room was filled with a stunned silence, and the implications of Sylvia's confession rippled through their minds. Who was Julie, and why had she believed herself to be Sylvia Plath? What had caused this delusion, and what had triggered her sudden transformation into a creative force of nature?

I returned to the blood marsh strip mall and found it dried out, normal almost. A hunched old man scrubbed the pavement clean of any traces. I recognized him—he owned the pizzeria.

He tried to shoo me off, but I was persistent. The exact conversation, the little feints, the charm, the building of rapport—you'll have to imagine the details. Suffice to say that in my persistence I gained the man's confidence, and he provided me with his understanding of the truth.

It turns out that the old man owns the entire plaza, not just the pizza spot. Every year, the seep begins as the calendar turns to October. It grows and spreads until the end of the month and then it disappears. Every year he fires all the plaza's workers when the seep gets bad, before there's a blood swamp, and he hires all new staff each November. Folks always want work before Christmas.

And during October? The old man, Saul, he also plums the secrets beneath. We agree to share notes, to plan an even deeper expedition the next time the crevices start to grow.

I ask him whether he has any idea why the seep comes only in October—and this part I'll repeat verbatim, which I can because I was sure I'd heard it before—and he said that October is the month when the veil between the living and the dead is thinnest. It was a line from that bizarre Sylvia manuscript. I felt a touch of vertigo. Saul grabbed my arm and steadied me. His hands had huge veins that I could not look away from.

Well, I told him, eventually, I guess I'll see you in October. Saul smiled, nodded. Better make it sooner, he said. There's much to plan.

When I arrived home I saw a dossier slipped under my front door. Notebook paper, familiar handwriting, a neat label saying Part III. It was the third installment of the Sylvia story.

16.

A few of the mouth-bodies, chests closed, sat vaping at a patio table they'd set up in the warehouse section of the Ikea.

"Do you ever wonder about your 401k anymore?"

"Not really. I was mostly in treasuries, so there really isn't much volatility."

"But don't you worry that your returns aren't outpacing inflation?"

"I'm more worried about the inflation of my waistband!"

"Heyo!"

"This guy!"

And then a couple in expensive coats wanders into the megastore and the mouth-bodies swing open to devour.

17.

Horse-sized mosquitos called *exsanguinators*.

18.

A schizophrenic with ecstatic visions seizing in the bidet display. *Delusionals* cavorting nude in the garden supplies. Paranoid barricaders erecting makeshift defenses studded with steak knives.

19.

Julie the not-Sylvia pauses in her manic scripting. How the fuck did these asylum creeps track her here? How have the mouth-bodies not eviscerated them? At least the creeps are just observing; there's no telling what would happen if they tried to apprehend her, to re-medicate, to restrain.

Julie stares straight into the Doctor. Mother paces, her long claws loud on the tile floor.

"Ok Julie," says the Doctor, "how are you feeling? Do you mind if I just check a few things out, make sure everything is ok?"

Julie minds. She says so. The Doctor persists. He lays his hands on her shoulders. Julie rolls her eyes into their sockets, lets her head fall back and sway. The nearest mouth-bodies quiver along their axes. Mother whines. The Doctor's hands move to Julie's face, his head leans to look closely, and Julie snaps her head forward with tremendous force so that the crown of her skull crushes the Doctor's nose and dislodges several of his teeth. Julie laughs. The Doctor falls screaming to the floor, where Mother sets upon him. Vicious. The watching mouth-bodies open and close, their teeth chatter. A new meaning for *belly laugh*. The Doctor is on track to bleed out.

Julie calms and commands a pair of her old asylum cohabitants. "This is unpleasant. Drag it out to the pond. I don't like to see his skin."

The Doctor's skin is, to be fair, rather horrible.

The professor wisely stays still and silent. Julie sits and resumes her writing. Mother curls at her feet.

20.

The professor really is named Sylvia, but not Plath. Nothing about her situation or surroundings interests her from an academic point of view. She doesn't care one bit about what is driving Julie's graphomania, the quality of her verse, the reasons she believed herself possessed or reincarnated or whatever it was she believed. No, the Professor—who we will continue to call by her title, like she's on Gilligan's Island, because to call her *Sylvia* at this point would be too confusing—is interested only in her own survival.

Outside the Ikea she'd seen mouth-bodies swarming—whole packs with matching Patagonia vests. She'd watched bodies flatten into their skeletons, skin as a kind of awful shrink wrap, as the *exsanguinators* buzzed between refugees. She'd watched the plagues of worm-bears and giant disembodied hands. Out there was no place to be.

In truth, she had more or less abandoned any interest beyond self-preservation even before the emergence of this particular hellscape. She had advanced professionally because she had more insight into departmental politics than any subject she ostensibly studied.

In other words, our Professor had always been well-served by her instincts.

Once the Doctor's body was disposed of and everyone around her calmed, the Professor slowly backed away from Julie and her coyote familiar, then she worked her way to the preserved Swedish food aisle and drank down an elderflower soda and a lingonberry jam. She stuffed a few more jars into her tote and bedded down for the night in a quiet corner of a largely neglected sofa showroom.

The next day she woke early to the sound of roving mouth-bodies, but they did not approach or harass her. They must have judged her insane, so worthy of protection. This brings us up to the present—the Professor realizes she is safe and nourished and able to choose between an endless selection of beds and pillows. Her jaw unclenches, she realizes, for the first time in days.

21.

I want to tell you a story—two actually. You can choose your own adventure.[11]

Story 1

I am not sure how I got here, but my name is Julie. I'm 30 years old and I am an aspiring poet. I say aspiring because I still haven't published much of anything, despite my best efforts.

Every morning, before I got here, I would look in the mirror and tell myself that I am a gifted poet, that I am the next Sylvia Plath, that I would pick up where she left off, except I, unlike her, will live to see my greatness.

I know I am not as naturally talented as Sylvia, so I have had to study and work even harder than she did, and I have had to dabble in a bit of black magic to produce my poems. I know that Sylvia had her Ouija board sessions with Pan. That means she didn't always

---

[11] If you'd like to wax nostalgic and read a few good Choose Your Own Adventure books, refer to *Who Killed Harlowe Thrombey?* by Edward Packer and *The Magic of the Unicorn by* Deborah Lerme Goodman.

write alone either, or I thought I should follow in her footsteps.

I tried to reach Sylvia directly first for writing advice, but I couldn't get her to respond to me. A spirit named Too Dark told me Sylvia didn't want to talk, and that I needed to respect her wishes. I was disappointed, of course, but Too Dark told me he could connect me to Sylvia's spirit guide, Pan, and I immediately accepted his offer. Pan told me he could guide me to write poems in the voice of Sylvia Plath, and that I would even begin to believe I was her.

It started innocently enough, with a short session each day, when Pan and I would write a poem together. Then it soon ballooned to several sessions a day, and I had compiled a whole book we had written together. I knew it was good, but I also could feel my soul slowly leaving my body. With each new poem, I lost a bit of myself, and Pan and Sylvia soon completely possessed me. And that's when the real trouble and terror began.

Pan told me if I wanted to continue writing like Sylvia, I would need to bring him the soul of a child. I couldn't bring myself to kill my own, so I went to an orphanage and began the process of adopting the oldest child there, and once I brought her home, I killed her in her sleep, and gave her soul to Pan.

After that, Pan became insatiable and asked for more and more children. I'm sure you can imagine what happened next, and how many children I have killed in my thirst for literary fame. I believe I will be proven innocent by reason of insanity and confined for the rest of my life.

Story 2

I am entirely sure how I got here, and my name is Julie. I am 30 years old, and I am a very successful poet—some have said I am the next Sylvia Plath.

Sylvia Plath was mentally ill. Her exact diagnosis has been debated, but I believe her illness fueled her creativity. To write like her, I knew I needed to reach the same mental state. I feigned major depression and mania at first, but the doctors didn't believe me. So, I decided I needed to induce the real thing.

I moved to London, married a brute of a man, had two small children close together, and managed to find myself in the same predicament as Sylvia. I would wake in the blue hours each morning to write. I convinced the doctors that I needed the same medication Sylvia had. I began to take it, and soon, it made me crazy, too.

I thought I'd be able to control my illness a bit better than Sylvia did, but it got the better of me. My illness was compounded by my mother's recent death, by what the authorities claim to be a suicide, but I don't believe them. Or maybe I just don't want to face the truth.

The guilt I felt over my mother's death overwhelmed me, and I needed help. I staged a suicide, similar to Sylvia's method, except I didn't plan to go all the way through with it. I figured this would surely land me in the psych ward and I would have some time away from my children to focus on writing and healing.

Like Sylvia, I had a nurse who came to check on me at home daily. I timed my attempted suicide so the nurse would find me with my head in the oven, but before the gas killed me or harmed my children. I was transported to the hospital and left a note behind stating that my children should be sent to a friend I entrusted to care for them.

I am now remembering what I had previously blocked out. I am not possessed, and I am not certifiably crazy. I am a brilliant writer with induced depression and mania—mania that can seem like possession at times due to my hallucinations and violent behavior. I also cut out my own tongue because, at the height of delusion, I thought my tongue was a snake trying to poison me. I know I will be confined for a while until I am stabilized, and then I will start this manic-depressive cycle all over again.

The authorities are still deciding which of these stories, if either, is true.

22.

In the heart of the city, life continued to bustle and move at its relentless pace. While the tales of Julie's two stories were being scrutinized, the world outside continued, largely unaware of the internal turmoil that gripped her.

People went about their daily routines, hurrying to work, laughing in cafes, and walking their dogs through city parks. The sun cast its warm, golden rays upon the bustling streets, and the city seemed to pulse with its own rhythm.

Families gathered in the evenings to share meals, and children played in the neighborhood parks, their laughter and innocent joy a stark contrast to the complexities of Julie's life. Love blossomed in the most unexpected places, couples walked hand in hand, and the city's heartbeat with the myriad of human experiences.

Amidst the chaos of modern life, the stories of ordinary people unfolded. The seamstress next door continued to create beautiful garments for her clients, finding solace in her meticulous work. The elderly man at the corner store shared tales of his youth with anyone who would listen, imparting wisdom and laughter in equal measure.

The sound of music drifted from the windows of apartments, as aspiring musicians practiced their craft, hoping to one day share their melodies with the world. The smell of fresh bread wafted from the bakery down the street, enticing passersby with its warm, comforting aroma.

In the park, an artist set up his easel, capturing the city's essence on his canvas. His strokes were bold and confident, each one a testament to his passion for his craft. A group of friends gathered for a picnic, reveling in the simple pleasures of good food and good company.

As the dawn turned to dusk, the city transformed. Neon signs illuminated the streets, casting a vibrant, electric glow. Restaurants and bars came alive with the chatter of patrons, the clinking of glasses, and the sizzling of delicious dishes.

The city's vibrancy was proof of the resilience of its people, who faced life's challenges with determination and hope. In the midst of their own struggles and triumphs, they continued to build their stories, each one a unique thread in the tapestry of the city.

While the outside world moved forward, Julie's narrative remained a subject of scrutiny and debate. Her tales had raised questions about the intersection of creativity and mental health, the thin line between inspiration and obsession.

23.

Julie's first story had an air of surrealism that both intrigued and mystified those who sought to understand her narrative. Her claims of being possessed by the spirit of Sylvia Plath were outlandish, yet there was an eerie conviction in her words that left many bewildered.

As her story unfolded, those who listened found themselves drawn into a realm where reality and fantasy seemed to blur. The very idea that a spirit named Pan could guide Julie's writing was an enigma in itself. How could one explain this ethereal collaboration that transcended the boundaries of the living and the dead?

Julie's confessions about her desperate quest for literary fame sent shivers down the spines of her listeners. The notion that she had adopted and killed children to appease Pan and achieve her literary aspirations was a chilling revelation. It was a narrative that defied belief, and yet, there was a rawness to her account that left a haunting impression.

The psychiatric evaluations delved deep into Julie's psyche, attempting to understand the origin of these disturbing stories. They probed her history, seeking any evidence of prior trauma or mental illness that could have triggered such elaborate delusions. But they found no concrete answers, no clear signposts pointing to the roots of her obsession with Sylvia Plath.

Julie's journals, filled with disjointed musings and cryptic entries, became a source of intrigue for those who wished to decipher the labyrinth of her mind. The journals were a kaleidoscope of emotions, from moments of euphoria to depths of despair. They painted a vivid picture of a tormented soul, oscillating between two worlds—the real and the surreal.

In the dimly lit room of the psychiatric facility, Julie recounted her encounters with Pan. Her eyes held a distant, haunted look as she spoke of their collaborations, her voice trembling as she described the sensation of being possessed by a presence beyond her control. Her conviction was unwavering, and it left her audience grappling with the possibility that there was more to her story than met the eye.

As Julie's narrative unfolded, questions loomed. Was she truly possessed, or was this a manifestation of a fractured psyche? Could the accounts of Pan and child sacrifices be the product of a deeply disturbed mind? The line between reality and delusion had become indistinct, and the mystery surrounding her tale deepened.

The psychiatric team wrestled with the enigma of Julie's mental state. They debated the possibility of dissociative identity disorder, where different personalities could emerge within a single individual. But even this diagnosis failed to fully explain the ethereal nature of her encounters with Pan.

The first story remained a perplexing riddle, a narrative that transcended conventional understanding. It was a tale of darkness and obsession, of a desperate yearning for literary greatness. The possibility that it held a grain of truth left an unsettling impression on those who delved into its depths.

24.

The thing about cities is that they hold lots of stories, and the Julie stories, in the context of a city's worth, are hardly anything at all. They are a grain of a sand, a drop of water, or less. A nothing. So, what if they dissolve, if they shear off into irreconcilable pieces, if they contradict? I contradict myself. Very well, I contradict myself. Foolish consistency the hobgoblin of little minds and all that. The multiverse, the unknowable. The sublime. What horror is greater than that? A thousand pages describing hyperobjects, describing phenomena that overwhelm perception— views of mountains from their base, the sea. The thing about stories is that they move. Or I mean they stack. A five-story building. A six-story building. Recall that *stanza* is Italian for *room*. If so then poetry is that much smaller than fiction; composed as it is of rooms instead of stories. Julie's stories. Julie's two stories, or three stories. Julie's little room with its padded walls. Poetry, that is. So, who's to care if the stories break off and break down. Trail off. Peter out. Which is what Pan said upon dropping his microphone. We return again to Pan. I don't care for devils. I find them dull and over-determined, too freighted with a particular moral overlay. No, the man-child Pan is infinitely preferable, prefiguring as it does much of the Judd Apatow & Kevin Smith oeuvres. To *pan* means to criticize via harsh review. What's more frightening for a writer? Of course, it also means to swing a camera in a wide arc, capturing the sweep of a view, which meaning comes from *pan* the prefix, meaning *across*, inclusive of all. Like an establishing shot, panning the city, catching tiny fragments of countless stories, swarms of commuters, hopscotching children. Those stories are just as worthy as anyone else's. Julie's already had at least three stories, plus the stories under her assumed name. Stolen name? Appropriated? And as we've established those stories are nothing, insubstantial, a fraction of grain of sand. So, we will leave Julie for now to whatever distressing fate. We will assume all her stories are true, all at once, even if such a state appears to be impossible. Hers, like the famous cat, are Schrödinger's stories, simultaneously true and false, or rather not quite either, suspended in potentiality. My physics are wrong, I'm sure, but the point remains, and the metaphor functions. Julie's stories are and are not true; she is and is not a murderess, is and is not scrawling unfortunate sonnets in a blood-spattered Ikea, did or did not kill children that were or were not hers. There is an awfulness running through the whole of her spectrum of potentials. So other stories then, in this bustling city. Enough Julie, for now, at least. Enough

Julie. She faints on a chaise lounge her torturers-slash-chroniclers set up for this very purpose of accommodating performative loss of consciousness. No, no Julie. It is time for some of the city's other stories.

25.

A story: Reginald the change eater did just that. Quarters, nickels, dimes. He'd hold a sign saying 'I'll eat your change. Any coin's welcome and then folks would feed him what he asked for. At night, he'd go home and shit out the day's earnings, pick out the coins from the rest, wash everything nicely. Then one day he got a little shit on his hand, and then he sneezed, and he jerked his arms such that the little shit piece flew up and into his mouth. He got extremely sick and two weeks later he died.

A story: Conrad and Louise move in together in a little bungalow off a courtyard in a gentrifying neighborhood. They overpay and under-inspect. A few weeks later they both die of carbon monoxide poisoning.

A story: A psychiatric nurse discovers that the ears of certain highly unstable patients may be carefully loosened and pried from the patients' heads, leaving tiny tunnels that, if one sticks a finger in, will suck the fingerer into the patient's disordered mind. Thinking it could prove useful in the development of treatment plans, the psychiatric nurse repeatedly enters these patients' psyches and maps the nightmare lands within.

But this psychocartography yields no therapeutic benefit. Instead, the psychiatric nurse becomes an art star and sells the mind maps to collectors for millions of dollars. Or the psychiatric nurse is driven mad by walking in the realm of these patient's awful visions. And/or.

A story: Robin catches the bus for the 1000th straight day. The bus driver blows one of those unfurling noisemakers. The passenger's Metro card had alerted the transit authority to Robin's feat of consistency. A local newspaper considers but rejects the idea of running a short feature. No one cares about Robin, at least not enough to read two to four paragraphs in the local paper.

Thousands of other stories in every neighborhood across the city. Horrible stories. Abuse and extortion and everything else, and ambiguous stories. Neutral ones. Even a few with happy endings if you squint.

26.

The mind-spelunking nurse was one of Julie's. Or in this thread of the universe, at least, a Julie and a Nurse Walcott exist together as patient and caretaker in a secure facility for the mentally ill, and Nurse Walcott happens to be able to unscrew Julie's ear and mind-meld with her patient through the ear canal tunnel.

Nurse Walcott, without patient consent, sneaks into Julie's brain, but it is too disarrayed, too terrible, full of strange dark rooms and awful flashes, whirling pages in tornadoes, yawning lakes of incoherence. The nurse is lost forever in Julie's head.

Some folks think Nurse Walcott is still alive, hiding out amidst Julie's synapses and ganglia, befriending packs of worm-bears and scheming to conquer wide swaths of treacherous oil land. This widely nursed fantasy is without basis in fact. If anything, the truth is quite the opposite. If anything, Nurse Walcott died inside Julie's mind, leaving her tiny body to rot and decompose into the folds of Julie's conscious brain.

Imagine the crowd when Julie attended the funeral. But no, in *this* Julie story, she is not the monster she appears elsewhere, or at least she's a monster of a very different type. In *this* Julie story, all the children she supposedly murdered were not really murdered at all. Rather, Julie coaxed each into her mind through her ear tunnel. And they are living there in a rather nice manor, growing older together, the bigger ones raising the smaller, pairing off as they age and claiming different parts of the manor, having their own children even, tiny mind babies whose cries give Julie constant migraines.

And when these kidnapped mind children sleep, they dream like any ordinary children, and their dreams penetrate Julie's mind and shape it, warp it, such that now it has an architecture wrought by interpenetration and accretion of thousands of odd, terrifying dreams dreamed by dozens of kidnapped children imprisoned in the mind of a vain mediocre poet.

And this of course, was not a pleasant place to be. You can imagine the sorts of awful creatures dreamed up and assembled in that poisoned mind, and that's bad enough, but eventually the creatures realized that Julie's ear tunnel went both ways, and they started crawling out of her mind and into the city. They started roaming the streets.

27.

I know I am, but one person and one person may seem inconsequential in the grand scheme of things, and among all the great and not so great people who have lived and exist in other spaces and planes of existence, and planets, but if I am a great poet, doesn't my story deserve to be told? Damn, that was a long sentence!

Maybe I'm not the next Sylvia Plath. Maybe I'm the next Marcel Proust! I'm shapeshifting! I can be whoever I want to be! That's the glory of fiction. Je parle couramment français, cher/chère lecteur/lectrice! (One must assume nothing about the identity of the reader. Why don't the French have gender-neutral pronouns? Or do they and I just haven't kept up with my French?[12] Yes, I digress.)

Autocorrect also tried to change shape-shifting to shitting. Is that because there are multiple references to shitting in this novel? I didn't write those! I have an aversion to talk of bodily functions despite them being

---

[12] Fact check! Google says: *The most widely accepted and used gender neutral pronoun in French is iel, a combination of il (he) and elle (she) that arose in internet and youth culture in the 2010s. You may sometimes see alternate spellings, including yel or ielle.*

very natural. I also imagine a literary scholar analyzing this novel and thinking excrement is playing some sort of great symbolic role. Maybe it is. You'll have to ask Beryl about that.

I love it when I'm watching a movie, and the author makes a surprise cameo appearance. Stephen King does this often. Of course, you have to know what the author looks like to recognize them, and how many authors' faces are known by the masses? It's not like we're A list celebrities or anything. So, it's kind of a nod to the true book nerds when the author appears briefly in a movie.

I also love it when the author him/her/themself breaks character and enters the page. It's so meta. Oh, let's not get too literary here. We wouldn't want this book to land in the literary fiction section of the bookstore. It will sell much better in horror. And is much more likely to become a movie that way, in which the authors can make a brief cameo.

Besides, don't most publishers only care about what sells? You know what's really scary? Most book sales and the royalties authors receive from them. Especially poets. No wonder Julie/Sylvia wants to be a novelist (Proust) now. Although Julie shouldn't forget that Sylvia is actually best known for her novel, *The Bell Jar*, which she published under the pseudonym Victoria Lucas. (How ironic.) Doesn't the general public love a winner? What is it that appeals to the masses these days? Well, I've just worked Sylvia Plath and Marcel Proust into a horror novel, so take that, general public!

Ooh, what if for my next trick, I drug you and convince you to tear your own face off? That way I can also work a Hannibal Lecter reference into this book. What if I'm not a real author, but a character in a novel who has escaped the page and movie scene and is plotting to murder and eat the rude? Who here doesn't love sweetbreads?

28.

Back to me! Isn't it always about the self with writers? People might be sick of Julie, but I'm not finished talking about me. If I am Marcel Proust, let's talk about my mommy issues. What really happened to Mother? (That note she left was so mysterious.) Isn't it time for Mother to bring me my breakfast in bed so I can write my novel in peace in my cork-lined room?

I love blocking everything out and being so self-absorbed that everything revolves around me and my writing. Aren't I more important than the average person because I am a chronicler of truth, because I'm good with words, because I am creating art and my words will touch others long after I'm gone, or am I just a navel-gazing narcissistic neurotic?

29.

This may be the time when I, Julie's doctor, come back from the dead to tell you that Julie suffers from Multiple Personality Disorder.[13]

---

[13] The term Multiple Personality Disorder was used until 1994 to describe what is now known as Dissociative Identity Disorder (DID) and is still considered rare.

30.

This is Julie again. I can see the stories you are telling about me. Don't think I don't see you!

31.

This may also be the time when one of the authors admits she has a hard time killing off her characters, even when they become annoying and it's time to let them go.

32.

Why do people often forget about Anne Sexton? Today would have been her 95th birthday. The last thing she drank was a glass of vodka. She died in her garage (carbon monoxide poisoning) wearing her dead mother's fur coat. We tend to remember people for their death more than their life—especially when their death is dramatic, especially tragic, and/or at their own hand. Anne won a Pulitzer for *Live or Die*. Sylvia also won a Pulitzer, but hers was posthumous. Fame after death can be more unhinged than the living variety. You're frozen in time and can't disappoint people as easily when you're dead.

33.

Who is more interesting: Sylvia Plath, Anne Sexton, Marcel Proust, or Hannibal Lecter? Julie has believed herself to be all of these people at one point. I find her most terrifying when she thinks she's a cannibal. Shall we go there next, dear reader?

34.

I wake up sometimes and feel like eating people. I know this seems strange, but there are people who take up space they shouldn't. It's the rude I want to eliminate. Some might say it's rude of me to eat them, but I'd counter that it's ruder not to.

My first "victim" was a woman named Rose. Such a lovely name for such a wretched woman. She had a laugh like a woodpecker, and she laughed incessantly until it felt like she was drilling directly into my head. I decided to return the favor by drilling directly into hers and making dinner out of her brain. It was a delicious brain for someone so stupid. I say she was stupid because she fell for my dinner trick.

I met Rose at The Old Library. She smelled like roses in the most delicious way—fresh and dewy from a gentle rainstorm, fragile, and blood, blood red. Rose was perusing the cookbook section, so I asked her if she liked to cook, and she said she did, but wasn't very good at it and laughed with a woodpecker laugh that made me want to kill her.

I told Rose I would like to cook her. She laughed and said, *You mean cook for me?* And I laughed with a laugh at a respectable decibel and said, *Something like that.* I asked her for her phone, added myself to her contacts, and told her to call me if she wanted to get together sometime.

Rose called me the next day and we arranged for her to come to my house on Thursday. I was anxious to kill her as soon as possible so no one else would have to suffer her woodpecker laugh again. When she arrived, Rose handed me a bouquet of the most beautiful roses. I felt a moment of sadness that someone with such fine floral taste had such an unfortunate laugh. It's funny how one small flaw can spoil everything.

I decided to make Rose's last supper an exquisite one: an assortment of the finest French cheeses, duck with cherry sauce, endives, a chocolate mousse, and a bottle of Amarone della Valpolicella. Unfortunately, we didn't make it to dessert before her laugh got the better of me and I had to kill her. I tried to drown the sound of her laugh in the Goldberg Variations[14], but even Bach couldn't morph a woodpecker into a songbird.

---

[14] Johann Sebastian Bach's Goldberg Variations, BMV 988: Aria da Capo performed by Glenn Gould and included on the Hannibal Original Motion Picture Soundtrack is especially divine.

35.

Julie's childhood unfolded in the quiet suburbs of a midwestern town, a place where the green of the lawns and the blue of the skies seemed perpetually at odds. Born to parents who, despite their best intentions, were often at the mercy of life's capricious turns, Julie learned early on that equilibrium was a fleeting luxury.

Her father, a well-intentioned man with a penchant for unpredictability, worked tirelessly in a local factory. His hands bore the callouses of labor, and his eyes carried the weight of unfulfilled dreams. A dreamer trapped in the pragmatic world of assembly lines, he harbored aspirations of an artist, an aspiration that often emerged in the poetry he would write late into the night, unseen and uncelebrated.

Julie's mother, a resilient woman of unassuming strength, juggled the roles of homemaker and occasional part-time worker. Her days were a meticulous dance between tending to the needs of the household and providing a semblance of normalcy amidst the tempest of her husband's mercurial moods. Behind the façade of her warm smiles lurked the shadows of her own suppressed desires.

Despite the precariousness of their circumstances,

Julie's early years were painted with a mosaic of simple joys and unspoken struggles. She found solace in the pages of borrowed library books, immersing herself in worlds far removed from the peculiarity of her own. The midwestern town became a backdrop to her burgeoning imagination, its streets and alleys transforming into the avenues of her dreams.

As the seasons cycled through their predictable patterns, Julie's parents grappled with the intricacies of life. Financial strains, unfulfilled ambitions, and the relentless passage of time wove a tapestry of challenges that cast shadows on the family. The home echoed with both laughter and the silence of unspoken burdens, creating a duality that Julie would carry into her later years.

Her formative years marked the emergence of an innate curiosity and a hunger for expression. A schoolteacher recognized the spark within Julie and encouraged her to put pen to paper. Thus, the seeds of her literary journey were sown. In the margins of notebooks and the pages of diaries, Julie began to give shape to the swirl of emotions that stirred within her.

Yet, even in the seemingly mundane, life's unexpected turns left indelible imprints. A sudden illness befell Julie's father, shaking the foundations of their delicate equilibrium. The burden of medical bills added strain to their already fragile financial situation, casting shadows that even Julie's fledgling words struggled to dispel.

Amidst the challenges, Julie's determination to elevate her circumstances through her burgeoning talent took root. The local library became her refuge, and the books lining its shelves became both mentors and companions. With each carefully chosen word, Julie's understanding of the world expanded, and her pen became an instrument through which she sought to navigate the complexities that defined her reality.

As she approached adolescence, the quiet resilience instilled by her mother and the unyielding dreams of her father converged within Julie. The tapestry of her childhood, woven with threads of struggle and aspiration, laid the groundwork for the woman she would become—a woman destined to grapple with the echoes of her past while reaching for the ephemeral promises of the future.

36.

In the turbulent symphony of adolescence, Julie found her own notes, composing a narrative that unfolded between the rigid walls of academia and the boundless realms of her imagination. The hallways of her high school echoed with whispers of potential, the secret acknowledgment that she harbored a talent that set her apart.

Julie's teenage years were a delicate dance between conformity and rebellion. Her academic pursuits soared, capturing the attention of educators who recognized the flicker of brilliance within her. Yet, behind the façade of diligence, she yearned for an escape from the confines of societal expectations, a longing that manifested in clandestine excursions into the world of poetry and literature.

The local library, once a refuge, now transformed into a sanctuary where Julie's mind roamed freely. The pages of classic novels and contemporary poetry offered both companionship and challenge. It was within this hallowed space that Julie discovered the works of Sylvia Plath, an encounter that would prove transformative, like an unexpected gust of wind shifting the trajectory of a paper boat.

The haunting verses of Plath resonated with Julie in ways that defied explanation. It was as if the words leapt off the page, intertwining with the threads of her own aspirations and anxieties. Sylvia Plath became more than a literary figure; she became a spectral muse, an ethereal guide beckoning Julie into the labyrinthine corridors of her own creativity.

In the tapestry of her adolescence, familial dynamics underwent a subtle evolution. Her father's health, once a source of vulnerability, now became a catalyst for Julie's determination. Her writing became a silent prayer, an offering to the universe for the restoration of equilibrium within her family. The burdens that had weighed down their spirits were now shared across the lines of poetry Julie carefully inscribed.

As she navigated the complexities of adolescence, Julie's encounters with love and loss added nuanced strokes to the canvas of her existence. Relationships blossomed and withered like petals caught in the ever-changing winds of youthful passion. Each heartbreak, a poetic incantation etched into her soul, became a wellspring for the verses that flowed from her pen.

The dichotomy of Julie's existence became more pronounced as she approached the cusp of adulthood. The expectations of academic success clashed with the rebellious urges that pulsed within her veins. The tension between conformity and individuality reached its zenith, and Julie faced a crossroads where the trajectory of her future hinged on the choices she would make.

The transition to college offered Julie the freedom to explore the kaleidoscope of possibilities. Amidst the ivory towers of academia, she embraced literature with an unbridled passion, the library of her childhood now expanding into vast archives of knowledge and inspiration. Yet, the specter of Sylvia Plath lingered, casting shadows that both inspired and haunted her.

In the lecture halls and palely lit corners of university libraries, Julie delved deeper into the recesses of her creativity. The complexities of her familial history, the echoes of her childhood struggles, and the unspoken aspirations of her parents converged in a crescendo of self-discovery. It was in these formative years that Julie, like a fledgling phoenix, prepared to soar into the uncertain skies of her own narrative.

The chapters of her childhood, woven with threads of resilience and yearning, set the stage for the woman Julie was becoming—a poet navigating the labyrinth of her own identity, entwined with the spectral echoes of those who had left their imprints on her heart.

37.

A Rose is a Rose is a Rose is a Rose. Eros is Eros is Eros is Eros. You get it.

So sure, I killed Rose for her laugh, but remember that 'laughter' is just 'slaughter' without the 's'. And maybe the truth is I killed her for more than just her laugh. Maybe it was her better qualities that really drove me... But enough of the *why*; what you're after is the *how*.

As I explained before, she came to my place. I'd prepared a lavish meal, ensured the ambience was sophisticated and inviting, and all through appetizers played the part of the perfect host. And then the time came.

We were enjoying the main course. Rose sat across from me. Enjoying is not exactly the right word. Or, Rose was enjoying, apparently, and I was anticipatorily enjoying. I was at ease, maybe too much so, and I let out a joke. I am very funny when I want to be. And this joke of mine prompted Rose's laughter, that tuneless staccato, which in turn prompted my slaughter. I smiled widely at her and in a single motion rose and strode across the table to her side. The laugh stopped and was replaced with shock. I steadied Rose's head with one hand and with the other sliced her neck from the front to her spinal column. It swung back on that remnant hinge. Spouting and gurgling. I drank from the fountain until her heart stopped, then I lapped greedily in the cavity. Bach played on the background, a lovely accompaniment. The rest of the evening was more clinical. I carved and disarticulated the body for maximally efficient storage and dining, ate a few prime cuts raw and packed the rest into the extra freezer I'd bought and stored in the basement for exactly this purpose. Then I gathered the spoiled and unusable parts in a doubled-up paper bag and burned them thoroughly. This still left a good deal of blood spatter that I meticulously scrubbed and bleached. By about midnight no trace of Rose or murder remained in the dining room.

That all sounds elegant enough, you must be thinking, but what about Rose's clothes? Her wallet? Burned and burned. And what about the parts that don't burn? Her pearls? The little diamond studs she wore for special occasions. What of her teeth and bones? For the jewelry and her blouse buttons and a few stubborn parts of her shoes I poured concrete in molds and buried them deep inside. Her teeth and bones are not yet discarded, but as I eat my way through the leftovers I'm planning to similarly encase the bulk of the *unburnables*. The concrete blocks will become the foundation for the casita I'm building out back. Short term rentals, I hear, are quite lucrative around here.

That said, not everything's going into the guesthouse. I'm planning to fix a few of her teeth permanently into my mouth. I've lost some over the years and have a handful of others that are rotted enough to need replacement. Thankfully I'm quite handy. I can pull my own teeth neatly and then I'll make a cast of my mouth to pin down the exact dimensions available, then I'll take Rose's matching teeth, grind out any problematic edges, and implant them as needed in my jaw. This will be difficult, but I have trained myself to have an extreme tolerance for pain, a steady hand, and the requisite dental skillset.

So that's the how, and now a bit more on the why, which I seem to have segued into. If I'm being honest, it wasn't just Rose's awful laugh that led me to select her; it was the way her jaw mirrored mine, how I saw her teeth seemed strong and clean and, size-wise, analogous to my own. There are other reasons, too. There must be. I may even discover and/or reveal a few of them.

I like that I will eat her, in part, with her own teeth. I like this sort of slant-autophagy.

I have special plans also for her finger bones. Her coccyx.

I will reveal what I want in good time.

Now it's a day and a half after the big dinner. I scan the local papers but there's no mention of any missing person. I walk Ted to the dog park and flirt with a sporty lab handler. Ted mounts an Airedale. I sidle up to a few other owners with smooth skin and the right level of apparent muscular development.

I prefer a lean meat, but not too gamey.

The freezer has room for at least another two bodies. I'm a very efficient packer.

But despite my best efforts and what seemed like some reciprocal lust, I get no bites and walk Ted home alone when the sun sets. I take a few strips of Rose belly I'd set out to thaw and fry them like bacon. Charred brussels sprouts and gem salad for sides. A glass of cheap pinot noir. What can I say, I'm a sucker for puns.

After dinner I give Ted some organs and a couple of feet of intestine. I've never loved sweetbreads. Ted isn't picky; he barks for more and paws at my leg.

I'm turning a few pounds of Rose into jerky so I can pick at her when I roam beyond the house. I'm also making a slurry of a few of her tougher parts to drink for the next few days after I do my dental work. Dry work and wet work. It's 8 o'clock and I'm half-watching one of those television shows that are ostensibly about dating but really about schadenfreude. Slurry finished and jerky still on the drying rack, I turn off the tv and start working—longhand of course—on a sestina about people with 'Christ' in their names (Christophers and Christinas and folks with the surname Gilchrist). I gnaw human tendon. The lines in my poem seem to write themselves.

38.

The omniscient third-person narrator wants to draw lessons from my biography, to see in my upbringing and education a reason for my later turn to monstrosity. It doesn't matter which reality I wind up in, which unforgivable acts I eventually partake of; in all cases my backstory is the same. It is firm, unremarkable. But I must tell you, speaking as I do from the authority of inhabiting myself, that there is nothing to be gained by psychoanalyzing the pre-monstrous Julie. And if treading that ground causes you to feel sympathy or understanding, then I'm afraid you are either wildly mistaken or monstrous yourself. You can crane your neck into my past, but nothing you find there will provide anything but fodder for post-hoc rationalization. Please do not try to humanize me, for doing so implies you think me inhuman. I don't want to be stuck in your mind in the liminal space between the human and the not; I have no desire to be zombie or werewolf. No, no. Stare at me, I beg you, as I am. Not as I was or as you wish I may have been, but as I am— totally unrelatable, opaque and evil. There is blood on my chin from a woman with a laugh of a bird. I scraped off the palate of her mouth and ground it into a paté.

39.

This is Julie's mother, Evelyn. I don't why Julie keeps telling everyone that I'm dead. It's as though she resents me. She has always been such a dramatic girl. I have tried to help her, but she refuses to see me or to acknowledge that I'm alive. If you're reading this, please make sure she takes her medication. Without it, I fear what will become of her and others. She can be quite dangerous.

I know you probably want to blame me in some way for the monster she becomes when unmedicated. Everyone always blames the mother. You must think I did something terrible to Julie when she was a child—like beat her, or starved her, or hung her upside down and filled her bladder with cold water, tied her to a piano, and forbade her from urinating while I played Chopin like Sybil[15]'s mother did. But sometimes evil comes from somewhere else—a place that can't be explained.

I did not abuse Julie. Quite the opposite. I may have

---

[15] Sybil refers to Sybil Dorsett, a pseudonym given to Shirley Mason by Flora Schreiber in her 1973 book *Sybil.*

loved her too much. Overcoddled and spoiled her too much. I doted on my only child like any good mother would. There was nothing Julie could want for. Perhaps that was my error. Loving her too much and making her life too easy. I fear she may not have developed proper coping skills. As a baby, she never cried without me immediately picking her up and soothing her.

When she started to develop odd habits, I thought she was just a very creative child. She scored at a genius level on early tests, and I enrolled her in a program for gifted students. The teachers there said she didn't play well with others and lacked empathy. At recess, she spent more time talking to herself than to the other children. Is being an introvert a crime? I, too, enjoy my own company more than that of others, but I've never killed anyone, and I don't know when, or why or how Julie's mind began to split open and let these other people in. It surely wasn't my doing. I was, and still am an excellent mother. Perhaps Julie will remember me again accurately once she is properly medicated.

40.

Do you ever think about the famous people who died while they were young and beautiful? I think that I will die before I'm 40. It's not that I am all that beautiful, but I am wise enough to know that I won't age well.

Aging is a horror in itself. Who wants to feel their body slowly rotting from the inside? The first sign of a wrinkle or a creaky knee and I think I will do myself in. I can't imagine becoming uglier or more burdensome than I already am. And I don't want my children to have to look after me. They will have their own lives to address. Plus, I would like to go out while I'm still at the top of my literary game. I really only need one brilliant book to be remembered. I just need to find the time and space to finish it.

41.

I don't know who is speaking or if I'm speaking or thinking. What day is it? I've lost track of time. I think I feel like killing someone else, but I'm not sure if I want to eat them. The thrill of the kill may be enough for me. No, this isn't Hannibal. This is someone you don't know yet, and I want to kill someone who doesn't see their death coming. Someone who would never guess that I have it in me to murder them.

There is a patient in the asylum named Violet. (I, like Hannibal, seem to have this thing for flower names.) Violet has a very low IQ and is extraordinarily trusting. We used to play Go Fish and I would always let her win. I think if I bring her Animal Crackers she will follow me anywhere.

I would like her to follow me to the kitchen, where I know where the sharp knives are kept. I was once allowed to chop vegetables after demonstrating good behavior. What sort of moron gives a psych patient a knife? I would like to cut Violet into small pieces. Make her into baby doll parts. Perhaps bury her baby doll parts among the violets potted in the planters the nurses keep on the windowsill of the break room.

My grandmother loved violets. (Her name was

Gladiola. Yes, it's a flower, but the name means little sword. My grandmother's tongue was as sharp as a sword.) Renée Vivien also loved violets. She even came to be known as "The Muse of the Violets" due to her love of the flower. Oh, look, another literary reference. I forgot where I was going with this. Oh, yes: Sweet, dumb, little Violet.

I never asked Violet if she loves violets. Perhaps I'll ask her before I kill her. Perhaps I will hand her the knife and see if I can convince her to kill herself in front of me. I'd love to see her cut off each of her appendages one by one. I also want her to sing "Doll Parts" by Hole[16] while she amputates each limb. Given her sweet nature, it will take more than an "n" to turn Violet violent. How shall I push her over the edge? Drugs usually do the trick. I especially enjoy inducing hallucinations or maybe I should hypnotize her. I especially love taking total mind control.

Violet, you are getting sleepy.

Violet, you are such a beautiful little flower.

Violet, you will do exactly as I say.

Violet, you want nothing more than to butcher yourself very slowly limb by limb.

Violet, you will confuse pain for pleasure.

Violet, I don't want to eat you, but I will save your

---

[16] This music reference may seem a bit out of context, but you will soon learn, if you haven't already, that time is a bit odd and inconsequential in this book.

plump skin to make a lamp shade for my bedside and a rug near my fireplace, so cut yourself very carefully.

Violet, you must dance to Doll Parts like it's your favorite song in the world while twirling around on one leg and holding your severed leg in your non-severed hand.

Violet, you will not bleed out before you have completed this task.

Violet, you are turning purple, and you look so beautiful when you're not breathing.

42.

I want to tell you another true story because reality is more horrific than fiction.

In the bowels of the asylum is a cramped room full of abandoned children. Children are abandoned for many reasons, but these children have one thing in common: They demonstrate, or more accurately, demonstrated (past tense), magical powers and have used their powers to harm others.

Gathering these children up for institutionalization was no easy task. It required a witch hunt Salem style but targeted to collect child witches and warlocks ages 2-12 who had committed murder. It's hard to imagine children as murderers, but it's much more common than you might think. The hundreds of children in the basement prove this. There are children who can kill with a single glance, looks that can legitimately kill. These children can stop a heart, set a body ablaze, wield a weapon with their minds.

It takes a very special procedure to deactivate a child witch/warlock's magical murderous powers. It involves sedating, lobotomizing and zombifying them to the point that they are nothing more than an empty shell. But before this happens, their powers are tested, and their brains are thoroughly studied. The children who cooperate are rewarded with treats and are spared their lives. The ones who rebel are killed on the spot.

The asylum lab is run by scientists smart enough to outwit the children—those who can avoid getting killed themselves in the experimental process. Contrary to his moniker, the most intelligent scientist is Dr. Dumb. Dr. Dumb and his colleagues are cloning these children so they can study them over and over from inception. Women in the asylum are impregnated and forced to carry and birth the clones. The children are removed from their mothers via C-section before they become too attached, grown to full term in wombs that mimic the real thing, and go on to become model children: models of how to manufacture serial killers.

There is one flaw in the program: Sometimes the clone children are not able to develop magical murderous powers. The scientists aren't entirely sure why. Of course there is the whole nature vs. nurture argument, but the children are raised in the exact same conditions, with the exact same DNA. One of these children was known as Hannibal. Hannibal carried the murder gene but did not develop the power to murder with his mind. Even though the math doesn't match up, Julie believes that she is both Hannibal the Cannibal and Hannibal's mother. She also believes that she is a witch, and that her mother, Evelyn, was one too.

Julie told me she learned how to torture when she

was on babysitting duty with the clone children. She learned how to shackle, how to flog, how to sleep deprive, how to drive the smallest of the batch to bash their heads repeatedly against the wall. She said this became practice for the orphanage murders that ultimately led to her institutionalization, but we must question Julie's reliability as a narrator. She often confuses time, events, places, people, and even who she is. Julie tells so many stories she loses track of which are true, which are fabrications of her imagination, and which are side effects of her illness.

43.

Dr. Dumb has prescribed me a new treatment today: hydrotherapy, but with a twist. The dosage is a bath of half ice and half blood, very precisely measured. The blood has been humanely drained from the still-warm bodies of the rebellious children under 5 who were murdered today. The ice is shaped in perfect large blocks bearing my initials, made from silicone cocktail molds. The ice blocks are designed to relieve the recent writer's block I've encountered. The children's virgin red blood mixed with the ice keeps me young. I must make myself a face mask out of the blood (Elizabeth Báthory style) and soak in the tub for a full hour. I'm touched that the staff has gone to so much trouble just for me. I do wish they would pour me a whiskey sour while I soak.

It's me again, back recording about my exploration of the seasonal thin place at the strip mall. It's nearly October so I've started up my preparations again for entering the bloodlands. Assuming the timing works as usual, we'll see the blood seep start in a few weeks, and then will be able to get through to the other side maybe a week later.

My preparations are as expected—a lot of thinking through what I know of the place, gathering supplies, a fitness regimen. I won't bore you with the details. I'm just recording this brief pre-excursion tape to set a baseline about my mental health and plans before the descent, and to provide an update about the strange piecemeal manuscript that seems linked to that place.

As for the first part—the last year's been fairly uneventful. I've lazed at a few bad jobs. I've lazed through a few half-hearted stabs at dating. I've binge-streamed a few middling television shows in spite of myself. I am like you, probably, or at least recognizable. I am of sound mind and body, I mean, at least on the scales on which such things are measured in our shared social context.

And the other update, on the manuscript, is that another section made its way to me. I found the sheaf of papers taped under my seat at the pizza parlor while on a recon lunch. I'm not sure why I keep reading the sections I encounter. I don't think they tell me much if anything about the world I'm trying to explore, or I guess I think they do but through so many layers of distortion and misdirection that I can't imagine I'll understand the relevance until my explorations themselves cast the text in new light. Still, I am trying to follow Julie or Sylvia or Hannibal or whoever it is as she flows and shifts and kills not exactly because I think doing so will be helpful, or at least not affirmatively helpful, but because I have the sense of dread that failing to do so is somehow dangerous.

44.

Dr. Dumb chopped off his thumb and stuck it in the water. I came around and drank it down and now I am the slaughter.

Sylvia salvia. Wooly Julie. Hannibal's animals. Nameless and shameless. Twilit violet.

Kids in the basement as murderous X-men.

The whirl the whir the whirlwind. What can I keep straight? Who? I mean I mean I mean. Mother, moth, er, mot her (her word!), thermo, thermonuclear, mothernuclear, nuclear family, nuclear, unclear. Unclear. Uncle ar, uncle's ear, thermonuclear motheruncle. Unclear unclear. The morass.

What I mean. What I name. What I am—en, amen, I mean, what? The morass or swirl, I mean a muddiness, an unclarity. Drugs or physics? or or.

45.

Killed again. Knives and children. Entrails arranged into an Aram Saroyan poem.

46.

What's the oldest anyone ever turned into a serial killer? You never hear about an octogenarian snapping and just suddenly taking out half a neighborhood. That was my plan; to live an unimpeachably upstanding life for 80 years and then go on my spree, but life has a way of coming at you fast, you know, and I found my arm buried in her stomach and the attached hand wrapped around the inside of her collarbone and I'll be damned if I wasn't a day older than 33.

The Jesus year, you know.

This was in the Julie years, somewhere in the northeast, New Haven maybe? I have flashes of memories when time unfurled instead of this awful jerking, when identities were fixed enough to cohere from day to day, years that could be grouped together under a name, a place, a stretch of employment.

Now I can't even hold onto the notion of a now, let alone a name, let alone something I might call an identity. I am dissolving, constantly, dissolved and dissolving and I suppose constituting. Contingently constituting, but still. What I have is recourse to the pronoun *I* and images that present themselves as recollections. And the walls here, when here coheres. I think the 'here' here is a place, is a now, a setting 'I' am 'really' 'in' 'now', but 'I' am not certain.

What I do have, certainly, sharply, are my kills. I watch them in my mind; I transit into them. Are they then, really, what *I* am? What I've become or am becoming?

47.

Suffocating a professor and eating his fingers, raw, to the bone.

48.

Bludgeoning a young priest, skinning his thighs, propping him up in the confessional, and playing a looping tape of breathing sounds and gentle 'hms' and 'ahs'.

49.

Spraying aerosolized peanut oil on a crowded train.

.

50.

In the Sylvia headspace I think I think of murder as a creative act. I think I think of it, in fact, as a poetics. A kill is to a poem as a spree is to book.

I am glad at this moment that I am not often in the Sylvia headspace, or rather that I don't recall that orientation as a dominant one, now, at least, as I recall.

Holding on to anything beyond the unfolding *I* of the moment is becoming, I believe, increasingly taxing. Impossible even, possibly. The moment, or my sense of being in it *now* collapses. I enter a mind palace, turn to a bookshelf where every spine corresponds to a kill. My kills. I pull them from the shelves, one by one, and search for a redeeming anything. The pile grows. The mind palace of course does not really exist. But the kills? There is a throughline, I sense, a grand ordering of the dead. My role in relation is opaque. Everything is blanks and shadows, puddles of melt.

51.

The wind is a wolf howling through the asylum most nights. Besides the tortured souls alive inside, there are so many bodies buried in the secret underground cemetery. Unmarked graves of experiments gone wrong. All women and children. Bones holding stories that will never be told unless discovered.

The gravedigger knows where all the bodies are, but like Julie, he has no tongue. He digs the simple plots all night long. He doesn't mind the work. It keeps him busy, offers free meals and lodging, and it pays relatively well. He likes to collect first edition books with the money he makes from burying the dead. He tells himself the troubled are better off dead. He tells himself he is simply cleaning up the mess of others. He also tends the grounds and plants beautiful flowers for extra money, so you could say he is not just a grave digger, but a keeper as well, and he makes the graveyard as beautiful as he possibly can. Some might even mistake the graveyard for a botanical garden since there are no headstones or other grave markers to signify that the space is a burial ground.

The gravedigger doesn't sleep much anymore—

which is ironic, considering that he works at a cemetery and the word *cemetery* comes from the Greek word *Koimeterion*, which is the word for a sleeping place. You'd think the keeper of a sleeping place would be better at sleeping. But the haunted souls call to him long after he has buried them. Some are so defeated they stay trapped in the ground. Some are so used to confinement they return to the only place they feel safe: the asylum. Some hover over him and tell him their stories as he digs.

One boy named Sam talks to the gravedigger every night. He is a sweet 6-year-old who was unjustly convicted of murder. Sam lacked no murderous powers. He was at the wrong place at the wrong time and the killing of a teacher at a nearby school was pinned on him. The real killer, a boy named Max, is still running free, pinning vicious murders on other innocent boys who end up in the asylum and later die when they aren't able to demonstrate their murderous powers. Rather than releasing them, Dr. Dumb gives them a lethal injection and has the gravedigger bury their bodies.

You might wonder why there is no crematorium at the asylum: Dr. Dumb does not like burning. He finds it wasteful and justifies his crimes by giving the bodies back to the earth. He likes to call himself an environmentalist. This is good for the gravedigger because it keeps him employed. The gravedigger's library contains thousands of first-edition books—one for each body he has buried in the night. His favorite is a rare first edition of *The Bell Jar.* It reminds him why his work of helping to end mental suffering is so important.

There are separate sections in the graveyard for women vs. children. There are no adult males in the graveyard. Dr. Dumb also doesn't believe in killing men. A true misogynist, he finds men much more useful to society than women. He also finds that way more witches are brought to him than warlocks anyway: Hannibal and Sam being special exceptions.

52.

Dr. Dumb loved Violet because she was easy to manipulate. She wasn't always dumb. She had just been zombified for docility. When Dr. Dumb learned that Hannibal had murdered Violet, he was very displeased. He never could understand how Hannibal escaped the asylum in the first place, and for him to return to murder Violet was offensive. This is a place where madness is manufactured. Voices from behind the walls scream all night to be heard. Anyone who has stayed as a patient, even for a short time, is driven to madness.

Dr. Dumb is lucky Hannibal hasn't killed him yet. Hannibal only pretends not to be smart enough to outwit Dr. Dumb. Hannibal is a gifted doctor himself—also a psychiatrist, with a particular interest in the mind-body connection. He has his eye on Julie and would like to give her therapy sessions. He would like to hypnotize her to see why she thinks she is him and so many others, to learn how and why her mind split.

Julie reminds Hannibal of a grown version of his sister, Mischa, who died young. Occasionally, Hannibal has compassion for a woman that isn't rude and takes her under his wing. Julie is his current fixer-upper.

53.

When Hannibal opened his front door to retrieve the daily paper, Ted's decapitated head was bleeding all over the front-page news. He didn't know what kind of monster would kill his dog, but he vowed to find out.

54.

I finally connected with Anne! She wasn't ignoring me. She was busy writing poems without the interruption of her husband or children! She says we must get martinis soon. I will head back to Boston. We will go to the Ritz[17], and we will need to find George Starbuck! Oh, I just can't wait to have drinks again! The martinis may not mix well with my medication, but it's a risk I'm willing to take for a good time.

---

[17] Care for another good book recommendation? Check out Gail Crowther's *Three-Martini Afternoons at the Ritz.*

55.

Ted came to visit me yesterday. (My husband, not Hannibal's dog). He looked positively grim. He did not bring the children along because he said he did not want them to see their mother this way. He says they are doing well considering the disruption I've brought to their lives. I don't understand why he always focuses on the negative. I have left them poems and stories to read!

I told him to keep my babies away from that Weavy Asshole. He reminds me that they are expecting a child of their own. Shocking that she can still get pregnant after all the abortions she's had. What an awful woman. Oh, don't think I'm being judgmental. I just can't stand that woman. I hope she has a fate as awful as she is for stealing my husband away.

Dr. Dumb says it's time for another hydrotherapy session. I'll tell you more stories later!

56.

This whole journey stemmed from the government's insatiable thirst for power and control, spiraling into a quest to harness spiritual forces.

One logical and reasonable reason is probably because the potential that can be unleashed by harnessing these spiritual forces would dwarf even the most powerful nuclear weapon known to mankind. It's an unfathomable well of energy, a force that could reshape the very fabric of existence. The government, driven by the promise of this incalculable power, persisted in its relentless pursuit, undeterred by the lack of immediate results. They saw this as the ultimate key to global dominance, an opportunity to control and command far beyond any conventional means known to humanity.

It was a venture shrouded in secrecy, birthed from the fervent desire to harness unspeakable forces for geopolitical supremacy. Under the guise of protecting national security, a covert branch identified children exhibiting peculiar, often inexplicable abilities.

These young prodigies were flagged as potential conduits to realms beyond the mundane, deemed vital in the government's quest for global dominance. They were silently plucked from ordinary lives, whisked away under the pretext of specialized education and safeguarding society. Their destinies rerouted to the foreboding walls of an institution—neither school nor sanctuary—a nexus of clandestine experimentation.

Dr. Dumb, a man of scientific zeal and unquestioning loyalty to the government, presided over this enigmatic operation. With a cadre of scientists and analysts at his beck and call, he sought to unravel the mysteries of the human psyche and its intersection with otherworldly dimensions. The facility echoed with the tremors of unspeakable experiments, a dissonant symphony of the esoteric intermingled with the macabre.

Within these shadowy walls, children—whom whispers deemed 'wizards'—were subjected to an array of tests and analyses. Their peculiar gifts, hailed as an unprecedented gateway to unfathomable power, were dissected, prodded, and scrutinized in pursuit of an elixir that could unlock the keys to global dominance. The government's insatiable hunger for control extended into realms beyond the tangible, clinging to the slender thread of hope that these young anomalies could be their harbinger of supremacy.

Years bled into decades, yet tangible breakthroughs eluded the grasp of the government's experimentation. Countless tax dollars funneled into fruitless endeavors, leaving behind a trail of cryptic data and shattered aspirations. Still, the custodians of power clung tenaciously to their elusive quest, rationalizing the absence of results as an inevitable delay on the path to eventual victory.

The facility, shrouded in secrecy and enigma, harbored the silent struggles of these children, isolated from the world they once knew. Their unconventional abilities, a double-edged sword of wonder and torment, became the focal point of countless experiments, each probing deeper into the labyrinthine recesses of human potential.

Inside the cold, sterile walls, these children, once heralded as prodigies, languished in the dissonance of their own identities. Their lives had been pilfered, manipulated by an insatiable thirst for control. Yet, amid the shadows, whispers of rebellion fluttered—a faint echo of resilience that refused to be extinguished.

57.

It was Dr. Dumb who gathered the crew unlike any other. They weren't heroes in capes, but minds sharp as scalpels, each with a knack for the uncanny. This group of thinkers and tinkerers delved into what science couldn't quite grasp—mysterious powers, things beyond the usual norms.

Their tale began with hushed meetings, where they pondered over a puzzling project, something that danced between reality and the unknown. These experts, handpicked for their smarts, gathered with a sense of both wonder and anxiety. Imagine, if you will, a mix of scientists and dreamers diving headfirst into the impossible.

First steps stumbled rather than soared. The hunt for special folks with odd gifts was like chasing shadows—slippery and elusive. They sought these chosen ones, kids with that touch of magic or mystery that didn't quite fit the rules of ordinary life. There was Harry, with a sixth sense that sent shivers down spines. Theo dreamed of futures; his nights painting tomorrows not yet born. And then there was Sylvie, who peered into souls with eyes deeper than the ocean's mysteries.

The beginning was like walking a tightrope in a storm. Their first tests dabbled in uncertainty. Charts and diagrams tried to make sense of the children's peculiar ways, but the puzzles stayed puzzling. You see, they were diving into minds beyond logic, peeking into a world where rules didn't quite hold.

There were ethical questions that lingered like shadows. The team wrestled with doubts and worries, their experiments tiptoeing the line between curiosity and right-and-wrong. The kids? They were guided gently, nudged into what seemed like innocent trials, unaware of the secrets they harbored or the enigma of their gifts.

Days turned into weeks, the weeks into months, yet the answers remained as elusive as smoke in the wind. The team treaded carefully, probing minds for hidden keys that refused to unlock the mysteries they sought.

58.

"Ok but hear me out. It's like *Oppenheimer* mixed with *Stranger Things*."

"But it's just a little unfocused, I guess, and derivative."

"Oh my god this entire studio runs on remakes of adaptations of comic books."

"There's an audience for that."

"There's an audience for *Stranger Things*."

"Yeah but you want to introduce all new characters in an all-new world that just *resembles* extant IP. But that's somehow both too original *and* too unoriginal."

"Ok, ok. How about this? Start again. From the beginning. This attractive woman, late 20s/early 30s, locked in a cell for a murder she doesn't think she committed. She can't be sure. She can't be sure of her mind or really her identity."

"Alright, go on."

"And these doctors come in, and it's very ambiguous as to whether they are malign or well-intentioned, or maybe well-intentioned but accidentally drugging her for no good reason. She slips in and out of what feels, to her, like moments of lucidity."

"How does that work? Like on the screen."

"Flashbacks I guess. Fades. Maybe different film stocks. Subtitles. We can work that out just let me go with the story."

"Ok. Keep going."

"So, in these moments of clarity or whatever, she can picture herself in these different times and places, like in one sequence it's this awful dystopian near future with cyborg monsters in an abandoned department store. And in another it's midcentury London. And all this is weird and disconcerting and she's trying to figure out if she's crazy or if the drugs are making her have these visions, and then also if she actually committed the murder she's accused of, and the audience is also kind of trying to piece together the clues with her."

"Kind of *Memento* meets *Quantum Leap.* I like it."

"Yeah, and then the visions get really bad, like terrifying, like she's committing all these increasingly awful, gory, sadistic murders. And she doesn't know why, and she can't stop herself or the visions. The lucid moments become a kind of pure torture, and the doctors keep coming and it's all very murky and, you know, full of atmospheric dread."

"I don't know, I mean, keep going but this is getting less, I guess, *fun.*"

"Well, right, ok. Yeah. But also, she thinks she might be Sylvia Plath."

"Nope. Scratch that. Our audience doesn't care about Sylvia Plath. This is an entertainment company, not an art non-profit!"

"Alright, alright, so she doesn't overtly use the name Sylvia Plath but maybe we borrow some bits, a few winks to the ones who know, and some scenes set in that milieu."

"Ok, ok. Nice period settings and nostalgia bits in a few of the flashbacks or visions or whatever. I can buy that."

"Ok good."

"Alright, so then what? All I have is this confused woman having murder-visions while a bunch of doctors treat her or maybe just drug her up maliciously. Where's this going? Where's the payoff?"

"I'm getting there. So, the hospital she's at is an asylum. Very sterile in a terrifying way. Sci-fi *Cuckoo's Nest*. And we're getting these shots of the halls and the patients—slash—inmates all stuck there, drugged up, locked up, sometimes restrained. Couple of TV rooms with puzzles. Anyways eventually we find out there's this basement or dungeon thing underground. And it's full of kids. And these kids have powers, supernatural powers, you know. Telepathy and mind-control and, like powers to move objects without touching them. And anyways, maybe because they are actually evil or maybe it's all the torture down there making them act out, but it's the kids who are beaming the fucked-up images into the woman's mind. Like she didn't do anything; she's a normal lady. She works in, like, some administrative role at a high school and likes bar trivia. But somehow the kids latched onto her as an instrument."

"Right and I bet the end is some big war between the supernatural but quite possibly evil kids and the originally well-intentioned doctors who started collecting and studying the kids, and let their egomania and thirst for power turn them into monsters?"

"Yeah, exactly."

"This is just what you pitched me before, but with a complicated and unnecessary plot about mentally torturing some poor woman."

"And…"

"And we're still not going to make it."

"What if there's, like, a frame narrative where this character is exploring a gateway to some kind of body-horror underworld and keeps discovering fragments of the main story that seem to reflect or foreshadow his own explorations."

"Still no."

"And what if as the story is coming to an end the two worlds start to overlap, like the explorer and the woman with the radically unstable identities who is maybe a murderer end up meeting on the same, you know, plane of reality or whatever, and that meeting is maybe impossible according to the logics of the worlds in which they exist. So, there's this lingering question of does this destroy or negate everything?"

"No, this is getting more confusing and worse."

"We could make it a love story?"

59.

I spend a lot of time in the basement with the magic kids. The doctors call it the *subterranean laboratory* and they call the kids the *paranormal subjects,* but I prefer words that tell the plain truth. The doctors use language to obscure and exclude, as a field of shibboleths and distortion. I bought up credentials in the same august institutions; I know how to parse with the best of them, and the way these doctors speak is inexcusable.

I'm getting off track. Jargon and double-speak are the least of their sins. Like I said I spend a lot of time don in the basement there.

I got into the facility by taking a job as the assistant groundskeeper. I left my education, of course, off that resume. I help with the grave-digging, the planting. I try to smuggle in a little candy, to loosen a few restraints. There's nothing else I can do yet besides gather information.

They're good kids down there, mostly. Or they are normal enough, at least, except for their powers. But there are a few, the doctors' favorites, who frighten me. There are six, in fact, who have been moved to special quarters, who are given privileges to harm the other children as practice, who've had their cruelty fostered along with their powers and focus. I am quite sure the rest of the children must be freed and given the chance at normalcy and perhaps some guidance on using their gifts. But the six, I admit, gives me deep pause. And it is at least in part because of them that I have held back on acting until now.

The six are not only trained on the other imprisoned children. The doctors use them to derail trains and force government officials into lewd sexual acts, to use mind-control over executives' family members for blackmail and extortion and insider information. The result of this program is a secretive fund run by and for the doctors that reaps huge profits by shorting stocks on the basis of foreknowledge of future events. It's insider trading backed by magic torture children. The doctors justify this as necessary to fund the program without government knowledge or involvement, but they also use it to pay for their own lavish lifestyles. I see them pull into the asylum in Lamborghinis and Lotuses and assorted supercars so rarified I've never heard of the brands.

And this is all awful enough, more than awful enough, but it is not all the six are asked to do. There is also a program of driving people mad in order to have them locked up in the asylum. These people, mostly women, appear to have been selected by the doctors. I don't know why each was chosen. I don't know why the doctors want them all locked up here. But I know the things they beam into their heads are awful. Truly, truly unthinkable. And these patients soon have no consistent sense of self or reality. What was a mind becomes a chamber of awful visions, disintegrating identities, piling scenes of hyperviolence.

Sometimes I try to speak with the women, to get a foothold on who they really are, who they were before. The conversations are nearly impossible, heartbreaking and chilling in equal measure. There is one, Julie, who I am trying to help claw back to some solidity, to a fixed ground of herself. And at times we seem able to sit in a present reality for a few minutes at least, but then the six renew their cruel mind-invasions, implanting gruesome memories that are, to Julie, far realer than the real.

60.

Are you ready for another story? Another man came to see me yesterday—this time, a dark, dashing man with a gentle nature. Dare I call him a gentleman, maybe even a gentleman caller? His intentions weren't entirely clear. He said something about wanting to help me remember who I am, which sounded kind of new age and sinister, and kind of sexy at the same time. You know I've been locked up here a long time and a woman has needs.

I may be reading too much into his interest in me. I'm like a schoolgirl with a dash of erotomania. How embarrassing! Oh, well. I'm sure they have a pill or some other treatment for that too. It probably involves a bath with some other bodily fluid I won't mention by name.

Anyway, this man told me to call him G.D., which I couldn't bring myself to do because all I could think of was that he was asking me to call him goddamn[18] and

---

[18] Autocorrect would like me to know that this word has been flagged for language that may be offensive to the reader yet offers no alternative suggestion. Are you offended, dear reader? If so, this can't be the first time we've offended you in this novel. And if you are deeply offended, you are welcome to replace the offending word with another of your choice. May I suggest grave digger?

that didn't sound right to my heart or my ear. I'm just going to call him Grand, which also starts with a g and ends with a d and sounds rich and stately, and even better than Grant. I like Grand, the name and especially the man. He thinks he can somehow save me, although I'm not sure he's all that well in his head himself.

He wants me to believe there are six children in the basement who are trying to use me as some sort of vessel and are driving me mad in the process. Why would children want to do this to me, and what is the significance of the number 6? I'm a poet. There's no need for a small army to stop me. I'm of no real threat other than moving you to tears or maybe depressing you.

I also have dabbled in writing children's books. Wait, are these children who have read my stories and are sending me fan mail via telekinesis? I really do think they should visit me in person, and I can read them "The Bed Book" from the bed I've been shackled to again. Won't that be fun?! (I love a good interrobang.) I can't remember what I've done to land myself back in this damn bed. I was doing so well in my Báthory blood bath. Anyway, back to Grand...

Grand wants me to remember who I really am, who I was before this hospitalization. He says I tell him something different every time he asks. I tell him, in this moment, I am Julie. He says I've told him that I am Sylvia Plath, Anne Sexton, Marcel Proust and Hannibal

Lecter at different points in time. I tell him he must forgive me. I'm on so much medication and subjected to shock and other barbaric treatments that I can't always know who I am or what I mean. He says he thinks it's more than what the doctors are doing to me—that it's the six children controlling my mind for purposes that aren't entirely clear, other than they are on a mission to drive me mad.

Grand also brings me a stack of books from the library and shows me his first edition of *The Bell Jar*, which makes me feel a certain way. And then I remember that I wrote that book and tell him so! He tries to tell me that I didn't write the book, that Sylvia Plath did, and I am not Sylvia Plath. I don't understand what is happening. I am so confused all the time, and I don't understand why anyone, and especially six children, would want to drive me mad and keep me locked up in an asylum. I am a good person. I'm a mother with two young children who need her. I know I can get well and can get back to my true self if whoever is interfering with my mind will let me be.

I have this nauseating feeling that everything I do and say is being recorded. Like I'm some sort of experiment on how to drive a woman to madness. I feel like I'm going back to the era when women were locked up because they became an inconvenience for their husbands. Is that what is happening? I just don't have a firm grasp on anything right now. What's a real memory and what's a false memory? Who am I with no sense of self? What will become of me if I continue to change personalities every few minutes? What do these children possibly want from me? Who is controlling these children? Certainly, they didn't become this way without malevolent interference.

61.

This script reads like *American Horror Story Asylum* meets *The Exorcist* meets *Hannibal* meets *Split* meets *Stranger Things* meets *Bathory: Countess of Blood* to me. Have I dropped enough attention-getting names into this pitch? No? Shall I throw *Harry Potter* or an animated feature in? Fine. Do whatever you want. Just start designing the merch and let me drop *Sylvia* back in for the indie lovers. Deal or no deal?

62.

Too much time has lapsed since we've seen a blood scene. Do we want another hydrotherapy session, or should someone die a gory death next?

63.

I want to tell you the story of another delicate flower, this one was named Lily. She was Violet's twin sister. Don't people love stories about twins and especially when they are conjoined? Well, Violet and Lily were conjoined twins, and you may be wondering why I left that detail out from the beginning. It's because I wanted you to hear sweet Violet's individual story without you being focused on her being a twin and especially not being bodily attached to another human being. And now I want you to hear Lily's, but I can't separate their stories any longer, much like they could never be safely separated from each other.

Lily was much more problematic than Violet. She couldn't stand her lack of freedom and felt constantly annoyed that she had not had a moment of privacy in her entire life. Do you know what it is to be connected to another human being...to never be able to shower or use the bathroom without another person present? To never have a moment of alone time? To hear the sound of another person's breathing every single waking second of every single day?

Lily had been driven to madness by Violet's presence, like Hannibal had been driven mad by Rose's laughter. Lily wanted Violet dead, but to kill Violet was to commit suicide, and Lily loved herself too much to do that. They were beautiful girls. Two lily-white (albino) dolls, immaculately coiffed and dressed, sharing a single body, and two white-blonde heads with violet eyes. To Dr. Dumb they belonged in the most beautiful cabinet of curiosities, so he created a special vase in his lab just for them, his rarest precious flowers. The twins were magical in their presence, not in their powers. Extreme beauty is a rare magic as well.

Dr. Dumb studied his flowers with great love and intensity. He wanted Lily to learn to love being part of Violet, but Lily was far too rebellious to be contained. She would pound against the glass until she bloodied their hands, and Dr. Dumb soon had to secure her and Violet together in a straitjacket made of bubble wrap for their safety. This only made Lily scream incessantly. When Dr. Dumb failed to silence Lily, he began the zombification process for the greater good: to preserve rare physical beauty. And now is when things are going to get very bloody.

64.

Dr. Dumb had lived up to his name. That is, his plan was profoundly stupid, self-defeating. The thing about zombies is they aren't alive. And being not-alive, Lily no longer needed Violet. That is, she did not need to not die; she was undead. And the same for Violet, though she had been less invested in living and dying and all the rest of it.

In any case, upon zombification, and no longer requiring conjoinment, Lily stole a scalpel from Dr. Dumb's unattended surgical bag (see, dumb) and sliced herself free of her parasitic sister. Violet stumbled away, missing key organs and badly misshapen, but undying. She dragged herself to a corner and slumped to watch the world. She had little other ambition.

Lily had cut the good parts into herself, nabbed a few extra organs as well. Back-ups, not that she needed them. The separation was bloodless. It turns out this sort of zombie does not bleed.

The bloody part came when our dumb doctor entered the room. He expected his perfect twins, that delicate sculpture of flesh that he had plucked from nature and preserved as art. He considered the twins a readymade and himself a kind of surgeon-Duchamp.

He didn't even have time to realize his art had backfired, that the twins' conjunction had been severed. Lily set upon him as he crossed the threshold of the doorway. She carved him up with brutal, desperate force. Stabbing and stabbing, shallow cuts and deep gashes and the scalpel driven so hard through his stomach it came out his back. Her fists tore into the wounds, her fingers spread inside, tearing all the ligaments and arteries, separating muscles into ropy clumps, pulling at gaps in the doctor's spine and ribs. She tore him, rendered him, confettied his organs.

And though monstrous, Dr. Dumb was not himself a zombie. He bled. Oh, how he bled, a deep red pool across the linoleum floor. Violet did not partake of the rending. She observed, silently, in her corner with her hand wrapped over her knee. But while his disassembled body was still warm, the zombie part of her kicked in and she began to eat. Lily joined in. Sisters at last, communing wordlessly in common purpose.

The separated sisters finished their meal and were not sated. They could not be ever again. They lurched out into the asylum hall, set upon an attendant, picked his body down to bones and another blood pool. And then they reached a wing with other residents. Julie, or whatever her name really was, sat with her hands on her head as a rugged man in gardener's attire sat speaking by her side. Violet and Lily locked eyes and started their approach.

65.

As Grand was attempting to help me remember who I am, two porcelain-white, mutilated girls with eyes the color of wild violets burst through my door and charged at me with scalpels in the single hand they each possessed. I'm so used to doctor's instruments of torture that I didn't flinch when the sharp twin blades came close to my jugular. Instead, I disarmed the girls even more than they physically were with a motherly interaction.

At first, I figured they may not remember me, but one doesn't often forget a mother's voice. I carried these girls for several months in my body. Surely, they would remember the sound of my soothing words as they grew together (literally) in my womb.

"Lily and Violet, I am your mother. Remember me? Come here and lay with me in bed while I read you a bedtime story."

And Lily and Violet immediately dropped their weapons and crawled into bed next to me, bloodied but still beautiful, and lay their heads on my lap and listened to me read them "The Bed Book." Soon they were peaceful again and spooning as they had in utero, each sucking a bloody thumb from their single hands.

Grand came over and plucked from his shirt pocket a single lily and a single violet. He delicately removed the thumbs from Lily's and Violet's mouths and replaced each with a lily and a violet, respectively. Lily began sucking on her lily languidly like a floral pacifier and Violet began sucking on her violet more violently than anticipated. Violet harbored more oral fixation and repressed anger than anyone had imagined.

66.

Grand called out to the artist-in-residence, who was painting a mural for the patients in the nearby cafeteria and asked her to come over. The artist immediately began painting a mother-and-child scene on Julie's wall: A vibrant rendition of Julie reading a bedtime story to her mutilated albino twins, with beautiful flowers from Grand's garden delighting her daughters' mouths.

Grand asked the artist to create a canvas version that he could hang in his studio. As gruesome as it was, of course he wanted this painting of his wife and children hanging above the hearth of his fireplace. It wasn't like he could take them to Sears for a traditional family portrait.

67.

My true goal in a place this monstrous is to make it as beautiful as I can. So beautiful that the patients, both living and dead, have peace. So beautiful that my wife wants to remember who she is. So beautiful that the doctors are so moved by beauty, they stop torturing everyone who is confined within these asylum walls.

I must tell you now that I am a bit of a magician myself. My magic is flowers. You may think this an odd magic, peculiar perhaps. But I can grow flowers so beautiful, they will stop even the evilest right in their tracks. And it is not just the physical beauty of what I grow that arrests monsters. It is also the olfactory effect.

Can I tell you a secret? Right now, in my studio, I am concocting a perfume so delicious it will place even the most powerful, and the most sadistic, directly under my control. Grand is not my real name. It is Grenouille. Have you read a version of my story before?[19]

---

[19] Reader, you didn't possibly think the author (the same one who can't seem to kill off her annoying characters) was going to stop making literary references just to sell a script to some Hollywood asshole, did you?

68.

When they woke, Violet and Lily stretched and sweetly combed their mother's hair. The sun was up and dappling the room through the window. How many years had been stolen from them all? And the twins were adults now, and zombies, or at least zombified, which meant they could not bathe in the sunlight's golden glow but rather had needs to fulfill. Those needs, of course, were brains.

Well, not exactly or only brains. That's a misconception, or maybe an embellishment, but they do need live human meat. So, the twins wobbled and dragged themselves into the hallway and down a series of corridors with long exposed fluorescent bulbs and blue and white plastic floor tiling. Being too slow to chase anyone down, they concentrated on the sleeping, the mentally incapacitated, the physically impaired.

They minced an elderly gentleman laid up with a broken hip, ate the face off a nurse's aide who'd fallen asleep on her shift, smothered and devoured a patient who had such extreme lack of short-term memory that they could sneak right to her side by stopping every few feet and hiding beneath a sheet.

Their parents, meanwhile, huddled in bed together and worried over whether the girls would make it back safely. Their mother was convinced the twins would be caught and killed, but their father reminded her that the girls had already been zombified so couldn't really be killed. Caught and locked up was a possibility though, and dismemberment, discorporation even. Dicing or burning, or both would leave them as scattered tiny conscious fragments, or so he understood.

Their parents needn't have worried. The girls were viscous, efficient killers. They lurked and struck without detection, ate their fill of fresh and still-expiring corpses, and returned with buoyant spirits and a longing for maternal caress. They crawled into bed—bits of flesh-chunks matted to their clothes and skin, meat-rot breath, blood clumps in their long wild hair—and snuggled against their mother. Much sighing all around. Another night to put off the inevitable question: how to keep together a half-zombie family stuck in an asylum when there are only so many asylum residents to consume?

69.

My success in saving my wife and children, and all the innocent people confined here, is contingent on my perfume prowess. I will need to create a scent that will lure more bodies in to keep my family fed in the interim, while perfecting the formula that will move the gatekeepers to open the rusty asylum doors.

Some patients may need to stay here forever given the gravity of their condition, but others could be rehabilitated to go back out into the world and enjoy a degree of freedom once again. I say "degree of freedom" because complete freedom is hard to regain once a person has been imprisoned for so long. For those who need to stay, my hope is that they will at least be treated humanely once the scientists and murderous children are under the spell of my magic perfume.

Any good perfumer knows that sweetness alone is too cloying. It must be balanced with something animal to attract the masses. In this case, a bit of civet oil and ambergris added to the secret violet blend, and a bit of musk and castoreum added to the secret lily blend.

I have been breeding, trapping and killing the animals that produce these scents for my special purposes. The whales have admittedly been the hardest to procure, hide and contain. I have been as kind as I can in all of this. There is also the greater good at stake. This is the thought that assuages my guilty conscience. I have tried to manufacture these animal scents in my studio, but like Coke said in those catchy ads, "Ain't nothing like real thing, baby."

I've done so much work already, but I need to perfect my formula. One drop too little or too much of any one note will ruin everything. It is the simplicity of these perfumes that will make people fall under my spell. Most desires are quite predictable after all. My two blends are currently competing to see which is more seductive, much like my daughters have been competing for my attention.

I will pump these perfumes through the air ducts of the asylum, much like Disney pumps scents throughout its theme parks to encourage people to buy more food and merchandise. We make so many decisions with our noses and are so susceptible to the power of scent, both good and bad. I will start tomorrow with a very small dose of the lily blend and see how it goes over, and the next day I will try the violet blend.

I prefer the violet, just like I prefer Violet. Lily is such a handful. Her petals are much more delicate than Violet's, who is a much hardier flower. Plus, lily pollen stains everything it touches this awful yellow—much like Lily is always pissing herself, especially in her sleep. She never outgrew this, and it's rather annoying to change the bed sheets every day. You must think of me as a terrible father, but most of us have our favorites. It's human nature.

70.

Once upon a time, there was a little girl named Julie. She lived in a cozy house surrounded by books. From a very young age, Julie loved reading—she devoured stories of adventure, mysteries, and poetry.

One day, she stumbled upon a book that changed everything. It was about a poet named Sylvia Plath. Julie fell head over heels for Plath's words. She felt a deep connection, like Plath's thoughts and feelings echoed her own.

As Julie grew, so did her obsession with Plath. She read everything about her, dressed like her, and even tried to eat the foods Plath loved. She often pretended to be Sylvia, saying she was her when others asked her name.

Julie's parents noticed something was different about her. She didn't just like Plath's poetry—she believed she was Sylvia. They took her to doctors, hoping for help, but no one could understand what was happening inside Julie's head.

Years passed, and Julie's belief grew stronger. She stopped responding to her own name, insisting on being called Sylvia. It wasn't just a game or a phase; it was her reality.

In school, things became complicated. Julie would correct her teachers when they called her by her real name. She'd recite Plath's poems as if they were her own. Kids laughed, not understanding what was happening to their classmate.

Doctors called her condition "delusional misidentification syndrome." It was a fancy way of saying Julie was stuck believing she was someone else, someone famous. They said it was rare and puzzling, and they didn't know how to fix it.

Julie's family was heartbroken. They tried to keep her away from Plath's writings, hoping it might help, but it only made things worse. Julie felt lost without the words that comforted her for so long.

Scientists and doctors tried hard to understand her condition. They studied her brain, searching for clues to unravel the mystery. But the brain, with all its twists and turns, held onto Julie's belief tightly.

Her world had become a mix of reality and imagination, a puzzle no one could solve. Sometimes Julie knew who she really was, but most times, Sylvia was all she could see.

Years turned into decades. Science advanced, but Julie's condition stayed the same. Doctors wished they could open a door in her mind to let the real Julie step out. But the door remained shut, locked by beliefs ingrained since childhood.

Julie's story became a part of medical textbooks.

Her condition puzzled researchers worldwide. They talked about her at conferences, trying to find ways to untangle the knots in her brain.

Through it all, Julie, or rather, Sylvia, lived her life. She spent her days lost in words, scribbling poetry, lost in her beautiful, bewildering world. And though science made progress, the key to unlocking her mind remained a mystery, leaving Julie and her loved ones in a bittersweet dance between reality and the extraordinary realm she inhabited within herself.

71.

Julie's mental state continues to deteriorate in the hospital. She starts believing she embodies not just Sylvia Plath but multiple historical and fictional figures. This perplexing condition puzzles the medical staff, leading to a recommendation for specialized treatment at a secure facility.

She is transferred to a high-security psychiatric hospital where she encounters Mary, a woman convinced she's Anne Boleyn, and several others entrenched in similar delusions. Julie struggles to reconcile her own identity amidst these complex personalities.

The institution's regimen of therapy and medication offers little solace. Instead, Julie delves deeper into her imagined personas, fully convinced she's more than just Sylvia Plath. The government's interest in her case intensifies, attributing her condition to potential links with experimental mental states. They propose her inclusion in a research program to study unusual cognitive disorders, coercing her into becoming a subject against her will.

This unexpected turn only amplifies Julie's turmoil, exacerbating her delusions and intensifying her distrust of the government and the medical establishment.

72.

Delusional Misidentification Syndrome (DMS), a perplexing neuropsychiatric condition, draws intrigue from both the scientific community and the public due to its enigmatic nature and profound impact on affected individuals like Julie. This syndrome encompasses a group of disorders where individuals misidentify people, places, objects, or events despite evidence contrary to their beliefs.

From a scientific perspective, DMS links with disruptions in the brain's cognitive processing and neural connectivity, particularly within areas responsible for memory, recognition, and attribution. Pathological changes in these regions, such as the fusiform gyrus and the right hemisphere, have been noted, leading to an altered perception of reality and identity.

Julie's situation is akin to a complex puzzle with fragmented pieces. Her early fascination with the literary figure Sylvia Plath became a catalyst for an intricate web of delusions. The intricate interplay between her intense admiration and immersion in the late Poetess's works and her subsequent identification with her unveils the depths of her psychological turmoil.

Neuroscientific studies suggest that DMS often coexists with other mental health disorders, including schizophrenia, dementia, or traumatic brain injuries. Julie's case mirrors this association, showcasing a multifaceted manifestation involving not only DMS but possibly an array of interconnected conditions.

The potential treatments for DMS often hinge on a combination of psychotherapy, cognitive behavioral interventions, and pharmacotherapy. Julie's condition seems to elude conventional remedies, posing a challenge for healthcare professionals.

In Julie's narrative, the impact of DMS goes beyond a mere clinical diagnosis; it is a life-altering force, dismantling her reality, isolating her from conventional societal norms, and placing her at the center of medical and governmental scrutiny. The societal and ethical implications of her condition echo through the corridors of both scientific inquiry and human compassion.

It is October again, and I am recording again. The blood seep has begun, though only as a trickle, a few small patches that the strip mall employees take turns mopping up. In a week they'll all be let go, the parking lot will be cordoned off, and the real exploration can begin.

I've got proper supplies this time—ropes and radios, firestarter, dehydrated food. Bandages and lights.

Each day since the month began I've parked myself in the pizza parlor and taken pages of notes about the seep. I don't know if you've ever read George Perec's *An Attempt at Exhausting a Place in Paris*, but my own practice was something like that—a hyper-detailed documentation of the infra-ordinary, an almost anthropological account, a field study of a run-down shopping plaza as it transforms into a gateway to, well, I'm not sure, but to something subterranean and alive and coursed with blood.

But I'm not making this recording to document the preparatory work, or even my observation of the return of the seep. Rather, I'm taping again because I found yet another section of the Julie or Sylvia manuscript. The section was spiral bound and floating on top of a blood pool at the southeast end of the parking lot. The back pages were stained a dark red, but legible and intact. In the pool I swear I made out the shape of an arm (small, child-like) reaching up and pointing to the pages, but I found nothing but warm, shallow blood when I went to grab it.

I read them in the pizza shop, in my normal seat, with a large refillable Mr. Pibb and an already-cold metal plate holding half a medium pizza. As always, the text was handwritten, and I've included an accurate transcription in the record, with spelling corrections and a few guesses at words where the writer's hand was unsteady, and I couldn't quite make out what was intended.

Except this time, I have not reproduced the last few pages, which were not numbered or demarcated as a chapter but were instead a sort of footnote or mid-manuscript sectional end note. What was written there was far too disturbing, too unnerving. I can hardly bear to think about it, and this attempt to describe it, or at least its effect on me, is proving extraordinarily challenging. Because in these pages, the shifting narrative voice finds a new mode of address, the second person, and furthermore it names me—my actual name, my accurate biographical details—as the *you* being addressed.

And this section left instructions, including the instruction that I was to share the instructions with no one, under threat of horrible curse and cinematically violent death. So, I will not share them, not exactly, though I leave this account of their existence. And I will follow them, though I admit both the steps themselves and the reward they promise terrify me. The prospect of not doing so—the particular and extremely specific torture promised (which I also am forbidden to reveal under threat of curse) is practically unthinkable.

Which is all to say, I will be recording more again soon, but this set of instructions and threat means I may need to be more circumspect in the next recording, as too many details may inadvertently reveal the contents of my instructions.

Ok. Enough. I have a plan to amend. The strange and awful will begin tomorrow.

73.

It is so lovely to be a mother again. Lily and Violet have taken to me like the hungry, vulnerable, precious little flowers they were as babies. They even let me nurse them with the blood from my breasts and sleep soundly next to me every night. Grand douses them in special perfume to drown out their meat-rot-mouth smell.

When I am unable to pump enough blood for my big-girl flower babies, I bottle feed them. I'm not entirely sure where the bottle blood comes from, but Grand always manages to locate enough to satiate the girls. He is such a good provider, and I am so lucky to have him in my life.

Grand tells me my birthday is coming soon and he is designing a signature fragrance just for me. Did you know he is not only a master gardener, but also a master perfumer? I love a handsome man of many talents! He also has impeccable taste in books and music.

He brought a record player to my room and plays jazz for me and the girls in the evenings a few hours before bed. I just love Miles Davis and Frank Sinatra.[20] I know some define the latter as more pop or swing, but Frank feels jazzy to me. He gets me up on my feet and dancing like a teenager at a school dance or a concert. That's where I pretend I am at times. I think I have found a bit of happiness once again. I don't even care about my writing anymore. I just want to spend time with my family and listen to records.

The hydrotherapy is helping too. I'm soaking in my bloodbath for up to 3 hours a day now. Of course I look like a prune, but the blood balances everything out. In fact, I've never looked younger. My skin is so healthy. It's like I'm Benjamin Button or something. I'm aging in reverse! Maybe I can become a spokesperson for a cosmetics company once I am discharged from here. I know it will be soon because I'm feeling so much better and maybe even closer to my former self. Imagine me, Julie the poet-turned-Cover Girl!

---

[20] It's been a while since we've had a footnote. How about another music recommendation? If you like classical, jazz, and old-fashioned pop, check out Pink Martini. Julie would vibe well with Lana Del Rey and Tori Amos, too.

74.

The local news just announced a major storm is coming—the kind that will bring rain for days and could drown all the flowers in the graveyard garden. I must begin to transfer the most delicate flowers in the garden inside my studio and hope for the best for the others. There is only so much space in my small living quarters, and the dark asylum is no place for my rare beauties to flourish.

Before he died, I had thought about asking Dr. Dumb to let me build a greenhouse, but I doubted he would approve the added expenses. Let's hope the outdoor flowers survive the storm. I need enough ingredients for my special arresting fragrances, along with Julie's signature birthday scent. She has been through so much, so I need to make something extra special for her.

I'm thinking of combining the lily and violet notes with ambergris. Maybe even a bit of fleece if I can find it.

75.

The garden is home to more than just plants. In my time working there, I came to know the birds that happened by, the sorts of insects that would frequent it, a few bold squirrels who'd watch me work from the top of the stone courtyard wall. But mostly I came to know the snails. It would have been impossible not to.

You see, there are hundreds of snails there that the scientists bred and bioengineered for their special diamond rasping organs (razor-sharp and nearly impossible to blunt), and which, if they crawl over your skin, will churn it beneath the organ to thin pulp and fine ribbon. And then they secrete a liquid that allows them to absorb the flesh-pulp, which fact means they favor bodies as food sources, given that they've been genetically modified for optimal uptake of shredded human.

Their rasping organs, which they possess in lieu of teeth, are equally suited to grinding down bone and sinew, hair and teeth, and the snails also efficiently uptake those sets of nutrients. This finely calibrated quality, and the mass of them when they swarm (can one call a multiplicity of snails a *swarm* or does *swarm* imply a kind of speed and motion totally incommensurate with snails?) means that they work collectively as an ideal machine for body disposal. I mean machine here, not just *system* or *means* or even *mechanism*; the snails are an engineered assemblage, placed carefully together and set in motion for a designated task. They are, in their collectivity, *technological* before they are *biological*. I think. Maybe.

Regardless, they make an excellent body disposal machine. In the earlier days of my employment, I would place the subjects here who didn't make it, whose powers were weak or non-existent, who failed tests or lost in the regular bouts of mortal blood sport the staff arranged as entertainment. So, I understood their speed and efficiency, how they left no trace of corpses. And I liked that they were morally blameless, clean and perfectly tuned, cute even, in the right light. I liked to watch their eye stalks work the air in early evening, their viscous semi-translucence at the magic hour.

Which is all to say I knew what to do with Dr. Dumb, and with the various others that came after to feed the girls. With the leftovers I mean. They wouldn't touch meat after it got cold, so I learned to keep the food-folks alive and incapacitated until mealtime.

I'm rambling or deviating. Deviant. I suppose deviance leaks out into all aspects of a person. Deviance creep. I'm doing it again. The point was to introduce the snails, the pulsing horde of them, the perfection with which they perform their designated task. It is even beautiful, in a way, if sufficiently abstracted. And what is also beautiful, undeniably, is the scent of their post-feeding secretions, which I am gathering and bottling, and which is indescribable and indescribably intoxicating.

76.

I know I've told you many disturbing stories already, but I figured one more wouldn't hurt since we've already come so far together. What if I told you that Lily and Violet were born as triplets? My third flower was a parasitic child I named Daisy. She didn't make it more than a day outside my womb—or so I'm told, but the triplets' birth was quite the miracle.

I still have visions of the doctor performing the C-section to extract something so fantastical you could only imagine it as a painting—a Daliesque creation, similar to "The Three Muses," but in conjoined-triplet-albino-infant form. Skin and hair of the purest white you've ever seen and eyes milky at first, and then irises darkening into crowns of wild violets.

My three flowers came into this world so tiny, a perfect 3 pounds apiece, and hugging as if locked in an eternal embrace, various parts of them connected to each other—each so dependent on the other for survival. They didn't make a sound when they separated from me and entered the world, and not when the doctors prepared them to hand to me. I knew they would be special, but how special was unclear. This was before the time of ultrasounds, when women just had to trust the doctors that all would be ok.

Drugs can cause many birth defects, but in my case, I think the creation was seen less as a defect and more a modern medical marvel. I think you can find us in the headlines and in the Guinness Book of World Records: "Woman gives birth to first identical, albino triplets."

My poor parasitic Daisy was too delicate to survive in this world. She was cut at the stem from Lily and Violet, and buried in a grave where Grand tends to her daily. You can find her headstone among the sea of daisies planted at her feet.

Lily and Violet must have been affected by the separation from their sister, having shared a home together for nine months prior to their birth. I was devastated at the loss of a child, but knew Daisy was essentially brain dead at birth.

77.

Julie woke with a splitting headache. At first, she thought her blood sugar might be low from not eating much the day before. Then she realized her body was low on blood from the twins sucking her dry during daily breast-feedings. She called out to the nurse, who quickly hooked her up to an IV of blood for the purposes of transfusion.

The twins continued to sleep deeply as Julie replenished her blood supply. Julie was happy to give this gift of blood to her girls, although the feedings were slowly starting to drain her. She considered the act a mother's sacrifice and Grand had even fashioned her a special martyr medal made of gold, amethysts and opals. He stole the gold and jewels from the dead bodies of the rich patients in the asylum before he buried them.

78.

A murder of crows blackened the sky just as the first clap of thunder punctured the clouds. The cascade of rain that came next was a surprise even to Grand, who had been forewarned. It rained for the next 666 days and 666 nights—much longer than the meteorologist predicted. Shocking, I know.

As the flowers drowned in the graveyard garden, Grand turned his attention to the flowers he had transplanted safely inside and took to perfecting his perfumes for Julie and the sadists. (Note to readers, Julie & The Sadists would be a cool name for a band, although Sylvia & The Sadists is more alliterative.)

As he extracted the essence from the lilies, violets, civets, beavers, musk deer and whales, Grand thought about the notes of fleece he coveted. He could think of only one person he knew who might have fleece notes and who also might be brave enough to weather the floods. Grand dialed Hannibal and asked him if he could come over for a glass of fine wine and to test out a new fragrance he was perfecting. Hannibal immediately accepted the invitation and made his way to the asylum via gondola.

You may be wondering why Grand would invite his

daughter's murderer over, but I'm sure you've already figured out that this book bends time. Grand doesn't know that Hannibal killed his precious Violet...yet.

When Hannibal arrived at Grand's studio, his nose was delighted by the fragrance that greeted him at the threshold. He slowly removed his bespoke rain boots and hung his bespoke raincoat on the brass lion head hook next to the door. He stood at the entryway and inhaled deeply.

"Lily. Violet. Ambergris. Very delicious. But you are missing something critical, and that's why you called me over?" Hannibal asked Grand.

Grand nodded. "Yes. What would you think about adding a few notes of fleece?"

"Who is this fragrance for," Hannibal asked. "As you and I both know, perfume must be tailored like a fine suit. It is very personal and must perfectly complement the body."

"It's for Julie," Grand explained.

Hannibal thought about this for a full minute. "I think I would swap the fleece for a trace of labdanum. Have you got any?"

Grand, in fact, did not. "That's a fine idea. I was hoping you might be able to help me procure some specific notes—notes I'm unable to grow here or derive from an animal, which is how I make most of my formulas."

"Well, it just so happens I am planning a trip to

Spain. I am low on a few essential ingredients I need for my own fragrances, and with the weather, the post certainly won't deliver packages for some time. Shall we discuss payment? I'm sorry, but I don't work for free."

Grand anticipated there would be a hefty price to pay. "I will take you to the restricted area of the asylum (aka the lab) and you may choose whichever patient you find rudest, take them home, and eat them for dinner."

"Are there any patients who aren't full of drugs? You know I need the organs to be as pure as possible. I am very careful about what I put into my body."

"There are, in fact, 6 murderous children, all very rude and all drug-free. Would you like to meet them?"

"Yes, very much," Hannibal said with a sinister grin spreading across his face. "Just one more thing. I also want the head of whoever killed Ted, my dog. Do you know whose head that might be?"

79.

Julie woke each day, smiling. She'd greet her family, chat with friends, all the while wondering. What did they truly think of her? She'd try to convince them she was herself, but their eyes told a different story.

At family dinners, she'd feel their stares. They were searching, questioning. She wanted to say, "I'm just me," but they seemed to see someone else. Someone she wasn't. It was a silent battle she fought, deep inside.

She'd pen poems in her room, her sanctuary. Words flowed freely; her heart poured out. But doubts lurked within each verse. Would they ever understand her, the real her?

In her heart, she simply longed to be herself, without their suspicions. She wished to be seen for who she was, without explanation. To belong, without the need to justify herself.

Behind her smile, a storm brewed. A storm of doubt and longing. But she concealed it well. All she wanted was for life to be uncomplicated, to be appreciated without misunderstandings.

Julie lived in a world where she was loved, but not wholly understood. It left her feeling empty inside. She longed for simplicity, to be seen for who she truly was, without judgment or doubt.

Each day brought a new facade, a pretense to fit in. Yet beneath it all, she remained tethered to her truth, her real self-hidden behind layers of uncertainty.

The world around her spun, whirled by expectations she couldn't meet. She longed for a place where she could just be, where her identity wouldn't be a puzzle for others to solve.

And so, Julie continued, navigating her days in this intricate dance between the person she was and the person they thought she should be. She dreamed of a world where understanding was effortless, and acceptance didn't require explanation. But for now, she lived each day in the shadows, aching to step into the light as herself.

80.

The once warm and loving home of Julie and her mother had transformed into a battleground of conflicting emotions and unfulfilled expectations. Julie's unwavering insistence on living her life as she desired, a life that defied societal norms and parental expectations, had driven her mother to the brink of exasperation.

Julie's mother, a woman raised in a world of conformity and traditional values, couldn't fathom her daughter's embrace of a lifestyle that was considered deviant and unacceptable. Her attempts to reason with Julie, to convince her to conform to the expectations of their community, had fallen on deaf ears.

Their arguments grew increasingly heated, their words laced with frustration and resentment. Julie's mother, overwhelmed by the weight of her own expectations and the perceived rejection of her values, felt her patience wearing thin.

One evening, after a particularly intense argument, Julie's mother lost her composure. Her exasperation reached a boiling point, and she lashed out, her words cutting through Julie's heart like sharp blades.

The once unbreakable bond between mother and

daughter was shattered, replaced by a chasm of hurt and disillusionment. Julie retreated into her own world; her spirit hardened by the emotional turmoil.

Julie's mother, consumed by guilt and regret, sought solace in the arms of her husband, Julie's father. She confided in him, pouring out her frustrations and fears about their daughter's future.

Julie's father, a man of quiet strength and unwavering support for his wife, offered a solution that would change the course of Julie's life. He suggested contacting the government, seeking their help in enrolling Julie in a specialized program designed for individuals with her unique condition.

The prospect of Julie being sent away to an asylum, a place where impairments were 'repaired', filled Julie's mother with a mix of apprehension and hope. She knew it was a gamble, a desperate attempt to force her daughter to conform, but she was willing to take the risk, believing it was the only way to save Julie from a life of marginalization and disappointment.

With a heavy heart, Julie's mother approached the government authorities, requesting that Julie be enrolled in their program. The authorities, intrigued by Julie's case, agreed to evaluate her, their decision to accept her hanging in the balance.

Julie, unaware of her mother's actions, continued to live her life on her own terms, her spirit unbroken despite the emotional turmoil she had endured. She found solace in her art, her creativity a beacon of light in the darkness that threatened to engulf her.

The day of Julie's evaluation arrived, and she was summoned to the government facility. As she entered the sterile confines of the building, a sense of dread washed over her. She felt like a specimen under a microscope, her every move scrutinized by those who sought to "repair" 'her.

The evaluation process was rigorous, a series of tests and observations designed to assess Julie's condition and determine if she was a suitable candidate for the program. Julie, determined to remain true to herself, answered the questions with honesty and candor, refusing to conform to the expectations of her examiners.

81.

In the present, whatever that means here, I mean, in the present of this book, if one can be said to exist, that is in the throughline that feels most present—what would likely be picked out as the present by a reading machine or artificial intelligence (which term is so degraded as to be meaningless, and which fact allows it to cleave to horror, to be the imagined locus of such a range of futuristic catastrophes)—well in that temporal space the ceiling of the asylum began to darken. It grew damp and dark and heavy as it spread. At first the blotch was just moist to the touch but before long started seeping blood—little droplets and then a steady flow. The zombified twins craned their necks and gaped their jaws. Welcome unexpected sustenance.

Days of this. A week.

And then scraping sounds, and a pressing down, and a flexing out of the blood-logged plaster. Then the ceiling gave way, clumps to the ground, a hole. And fingers, your fingers, wriggling in the air above the awful twins.

I lied before. Or I was imprecise. This is not in the present, neither the present of your life nor the present of the book. It is in the near future. The almost present or just past present. It has not happened, but it will. It will have happened. Forgive me, my time slips. The smell here makes it hard to concentrate, and the time refuses to stand still.

There is still some time to go though. Even in the timeline written here, the die has not been fully cast. Your arm has not completely broken through, your body remains mostly in the world outside, in the pizza shop most likely. You have not pierced the veil between any worlds; the murder twins have not yet set upon your body with knives and teeth. In the timeline you're experiencing, you have not yet even made any of a series of terrible errors. But still, you must follow the instructions, and doing so will inevitably bring you to this point. Emerging, I mean, blood-sheathed, through peeling plaster ceiling above a high-security ward for the severely disturbed.

So, this temporal disjunction should give no great comfort. It is more akin to a bubble, a pause, a tiny sliver of breathing room before the guillotine falls. You are to die, imminently, in a disgusting and very painful manner unless somehow you can overcome the twins. You are not so capable. You are not so capable, I mean, of anything. You are worthless, a waste of organs and bones.

82.

Julie, Darling, it's your mother. Can you hear me?

Yes, Mother.

Tell me, what do you see?

A mouth full of mums—
flowers and silence
a frosted field that opens
into spring

83.

Sometimes, when I first wake from a deep sleep, I hear my mother's voice and think she must still be alive.

I've tried to discuss my mother's whereabouts with Grand, but he never gives me a straight answer. If he wants me to remember who I am, why does he keep my mother's existence a mystery to me?

When I am freed from here, I will solve this mystery. I know it will be a fresh start, a real rebirth, a true spring.

84.

Julie's mother is a horrible person—an energy vampire and an abusive narcissist who helped create the fragile mental state Julie finds herself in today. What sort of mother has her own daughter committed to an asylum? I know I am no Father of the Year, but I provide for my daughters and am doing what I can to try to break them, and Julie, out of here.

It's better for Julie if her mother stays far away from her, and for Lily and Violet, and for me too. These are three grown women who should be able to decide for themselves, and they have been involuntarily incarcerated here for large chunks of their lives for the purposes of scientific experimentation. They are being treated no better than lab rats, and perhaps much worse. Lily and Violet have never seen the light of day, and Julie can hardly remember what it is to bask in it.

85.

Hannibal made his way to Spain to procure the perfume ingredients he and Grand needed for their latest scents. He then hurriedly made his way back home so he could make the trade and gain entryway into the lab to choose his fresh cut of meat. (He had really wanted to make a stop in Florence, but his schedule did not permit it this time around.) Hannibal hadn't eaten a small child before and doubted he could find one rude enough to merit killing and eating at such a young age. Grand seemed to be a man of his word though, so Hannibal trusted that the rushed trip would be worth the reward when he returned. Besides, he had one meal of authentic Valencian paella with rabbit, which was indeed gamey. But Hannibal was already tired of eating animals and was ready for human consumption again.

86.

Hannibal loaded up his gondola with the supplies Grand had requested and made his way over to Grand's studio on asylum grounds. It was a long trek in the torrential rain, but Hannibal didn't mind it. In fact, the smell of the cold, constant downpour was rather invigorating. Hannibal imagined the petrichor that he would delight in when the rain finally stopped.

87.

While I still have your attention, I want to tell you one final story. There are many who have lived in this asylum all their lives and know no other reality, and then there are women, like me, who have been committed by family members, to whom they have become a nuisance. It is the ultimate betrayal to realize that you are unwanted by the person who birthed you. And it is another form of betrayal to realize that your husband was a conspirator and/or complacent in the matter.

Don't think I'm as naive as I may seem. As my memory slowly returns, I realize that Grand has taken a devoted interest in helping me remember my past so that he can help reframe my reality. He is not the benevolent man he may seem, and he may not even be named Grand. A man who agrees to allow his wife and children to stay committed here for so long does not live up to that name. He may not know, but I know that he is friends with Hannibal, and I know that Hannibal is a killer, some say a cannibal even.

One night when "Grand" came into my room to deliver the blood bottles for our flower babies, I noticed an extra peculiar smell on his breath—a smell I can only describe as raw human meat—specifically, a human heart. When questioned, "Grand" said he was experimenting with hearts of the dead to make true heart notes in his perfumes. But something about these heart notes on his breath seemed too alive, as though the hearts were still beating under his tongue.

I later discovered while nursing Lily, who never was good at keeping secrets, that "Grand" had taken to eating the organs of the people he had murdered to make blood bottles to keep his daughters alive. I can't necessarily say I blame him given the reduced food rations caused by the flooding. "Grand" was hungry and he, too, needed to eat. I thought we had been eating venison, as he had been breeding musk deer for his perfume, as this was how he explained the gamey taste of the food he brought me. However, it turns out we had been eating other asylum patients all along.

88.

And this is where the main story ends—abruptly like a sudden soundtrack stop in a movie for added emphasis, a literary form of Musicalis Interruptus. And this is where Hannibal's gondola capsizes in the tidal wave on his way home, killing him and the murderous child he had planned to eat for dinner that very night. And this is where Grand learns that the labdanum Hannibal brought from Spain is tainted and poisons Grand's precious perfumes. And this is where Grand falls into a deep depression, knowing he will not be able to surprise Julie with a signature scent on her birthday or save her and his girls. And this is where Grand takes to navel-gazing as a hobby, blocking out the entire world around him. And this is where Julie becomes so preoccupied with trying to keep herself and her flower babies fed, that she does not see the true writing on the wall—that the rain will never end. And this is where the flood enters the asylum walls and drowns not only the flowers, but every breathing creature left inside. And this is where even the dead die again and the undead continue to die. And this is where the rising water says, "I tried to tell you so."

* * *

Check, check. Ok, it's me again. Recording as I walk. The seep deepened and I pried my way beneath as planned. Lots of mapping and careful way-making in the blood caverns. I am tracing the same route as last time. I pick up more pages of the bonkers manuscript at the same spot and read it by the fire after I make camp for the night. This time I'm not coming up until the month nears its end. I'd stay even longer but I'll need to surface before the passage between the worlds grows thick again.

The new section of the manuscript does not frighten or deter me, nor do any of the other parts. I have my instructions, a path to take, a grand adventure for once in this otherwise altogether crushing life.

I have spent the rest of my time on earth vacillating mostly between being a source of mild pride and slightly less mild disappointment. I am, at core, *basic*, despite my pretensions.

But this is different and given my deep constitutive mediocrity it is no wonder I am so drawn to this quest that has fallen into my lap.

I spend two days scrambling over the rocky ground, wading through various blood lakes and rivers, hacking my way through the peachy membranous film that blocks the path every few hundred yards. I chant the incantations that were provided in the book, the ones from the page I won't read into the record, which talk of things unfit for polite company. Worm bears call in the distance. A mouth-body flutters by, eats a family of rabbits and spits the bones (chunked and sharded) into my face and chest.

Bruises, a handful of cuts. I disinfect after the mouth-body whirls off.

There are rabbits here. I forgot to mention that. There are rabbits everywhere here, swimming in the blood, back-stroking, idling on the shore by patches of grass. And the rabbits are of all different kinds, with differently shaped ears, different thickness and coarseness of fur, different ear shapes and lengths and weights. I don't know enough about rabbits to say the right describing words, the breed names and subspecies. They are all the same color though, the same tawny gold fading to auburn.

Anyways, enough about the rabbits. I see them, constantly, and they ignore me. Even when I pet them they go on lounging and eating as if I'm not there.

Really, this time, enough about the rabbits. My point is that it's day three of the expedition and I reach the ladder I was promised, a massive wooden ladder plunging into a semi-circle that appears perfectly cut out of the earth, and I take it down a level.

At the second level there are nothing but abandoned middle class houses and brine-filled glass jars. Four hours more and I reach another semi-circle, another ladder.

On the third level I watch a couple of rhinoceroses with machine guns walk by and shoot up a bakery. I take another ladder. And another.

Everything is as promised, a fact I find both comforting and upsetting.

Eventually I reach the ladder to the asylum roof. I am exhausted and not yet ready to confront that world. The twins will have to wait. I set up camp, heat up a can of Spaghetti-O's. I'm going to sign off now and try to get some sleep. I'll record again when I wake. Hopefully that will be morning. I pull out a rabbit I'd stuffed in my pocket for company and tell him to keep watch. He lazes by the fire. I tell him Goodnight and I'm telling you Goodnight. Ok. Ok. Bye.

89.

Julie, once a vibrant soul, a kaleidoscope of colors and emotions, now found herself confined within the sterile walls of the government facility, her existence reduced to a mere shadow of its former self.

The evaluation process had transformed her into a specimen, an enigma to be solved, a deviation to be rectified. Each test, each probing question, felt like a violation, a trespass into the sanctity of her mind.

Julie's resistance, once as resolute as the mountains against the relentless battering of the wind, began to crumble under the incessant pressure of isolation and conformity. The monotonous rhythm of her existence, devoid of the vibrancy that once defined her, chipped away at her spirit, leaving her vulnerable to the insidious whispers of the asylum's authority.

In a moment of weakness, a desperate plea for acceptance, Julie whispered her consent to the 'rehabilitation' treatments. She allowed them to pry into the depths of her mind, to dissect her thoughts and emotions, to mold her into a form deemed acceptable by their rigid standards.

The treatments, a blur of intrusive procedures, experimental drugs, and relentless conditioning, were akin to a relentless sculptor chipping away at a once magnificent statue, reducing it to a mere shadow of its former glory. With each passing day, Julie felt her individuality slipping away, her essence dissolving into a pale imitation of the person she once was.

The world beyond the asylum walls, once a canvas of endless possibilities, now faded into a distant haze, a memory of a life she could no longer grasp. Julie, once a fiery spirit, a rebel against the constraints of societal norms, was now a mere flicker in the darkness, her true self buried beneath the weight of conformity.

Her mother, her heart heavy with guilt and a desperate longing to see her daughter "normal," continued to visit the asylum, her eyes reflecting the agony of a parent witnessing the systematic erasure of their child's individuality.

The asylum, a place conceived with the noble intention of healing, had become Julie's prison, a compartment of madness where her spirit was systematically extinguished, her identity erased, her story left hanging in the air, an unresolved mystery with no logical end.

Science, with its arsenal of tools and its unwavering belief in empirical truths, had failed to decipher the extent of the mirage that was Julie's reality. Its rigid frameworks and methodologies were ill-equipped to navigate the fluid, ever-shifting landscapes of her mind.

Me again. Morning. And a good morning. The rabbit stayed put in camp, so I scooped him (or her? I can't tell with rabbits) up and re-pocketed him (her?). And I know I promised to begin recording first thing but well, one, I'm not sure anyone will ever hear this and, two, I'm the one exploring and can take some liberties with my own rules. I found another scrap of manuscript last night. I'm not sure if I have the whole book (book? can you call it that), nor am I sure I've read the thing in order, nor do I know the order everything is meant to be in. I've added chapter numbers for my own benefit, to facilitate returning to sections and keep things straight in my head, but really I don't know what goes where, just that the whole thing is written in the same shaky hand and keeps returning to the same characters and places and gore, so I am confident it all belongs together in some way or another. Anyway, I read the new pages into the record and tucked them into the pocket with the bunny, which was maybe a mistake because I can hear the nibbling as I record this.

And other than that, I've broken camp and returned my supplies to my pack. It's time to descend the ladder. I am climbing onto it now, and heading down, down, and yes, I see where the ladder cuts off a foot or so above the asylum roof. It's a few minutes away. I'm descending.

I am on the roof. The landing was a bit tricky; the roof is slate and set at a gentle-enough grade but still sloping downward, so not easy to land on neatly when carrying, as I am, an overly heavy pack and a small pocket rabbit.

I know the steps I have to count, the spot to break through, and I go there and hope whoever transcribes this recording, if it isn't me, will edit out all the huffing and cursing I'm doing because it's not really relevant or interesting to anyone trying to follow my account of this quest or adventure or whatever.

So, ok I am pounding on the roof at the spot, and I can feel it is giving way, and I break through and lower myself from the outer roof to the crawl space between the slanted slate roof and the flat interior drywall ceilings. I make my way, as instructed, along the wooden beam in the crawl space until I again hit my designated mark.

I am being a bit cryptic about exact locations and the particular language of the instructions, given the threats made therein about over-revealing, so I apologize for the lack of specificity here, for the blunt dull descriptions of action. I am trying to keep you, the listener, I mean the recording, current as I move, but also trying to move quickly, so it's tough to balance the thinking of the narration, or even what details matter, with the kind of pure forward-going momentum required of the task, and anyways I'm now feeling my fingertips wriggling in the clear air of the room beneath the flat drywall ceiling where I've been instructed to dig.

And now my arm is through, and the hole is wide enough, and I look down and sure enough there the rotting disconjoined twins stare up at me.

So, I am pausing. I think or know that I am supposed to drop to them, but why? Am I a sacrifice? Do I want to be eaten alive by the dead? Fuck it. I'm here and they are beneath, and the instructions instructed. I am fall—

ENDNOTES

Ambergris

Ambergris is beautiful word from the Latin *ambra grisea* and the Old French *ambre gris* for what is rather unbeautifully described as a waxy, flammable substance of a dull grey or blackish color produced in the digestive system of sperm whales (read whale vomit or shit, depending on the source.) Freshly produced ambergris has a marine, fecal odor and develops a sweet, earthy scent as it ages. It is highly valued by perfume makers, although it has mostly been replaced by a synthetic due to its prohibitive cost (hence the moniker "floating gold"). Dogs are sometimes used to hunt ambergris given their attraction to the smell, much like hogs are used to hunt truffles. It is noteworthy that virtually all dogs can be trained to hunt truffles as well. Given the great nose dogs have, Nicole Tallman thinks about the types of perfume they would create if they had the proper tools.

Beryl Cooper

Beryl Cooper is not a real person. What kind of a name is Beryl Cooper anyways? It's really contrived, and the pun is too cute by half. But the nice part about 'ol Beryl is that the name is ambivalent about its gender, age, place of origin even. In much of the world, Beryl is a squarely female name, but in the United States it is a unisex name, possibly even leaning toward being predominantly male, so much so that at least one prominent writer of horror fiction has used it as the first name of a pseudonym in recent years. Beryl Cooper is the sort of name that builds in a homophonic redundancy, a stutter, like Candle Candlemaker. And it means the person who makes round empty containers, sturdy enough, and certainly an object reflecting craft, but hollow by design. Beryl Cooper is thus a sort of vacuum-ghost, producer of emptiness, ornamenter of hollows. Where you read the sections attributed, remember this. Remember that a real person is hiding behind the name, using it as a shield so the name can append itself to filth, and think about the filth your own name keeps you from expressing. The filth is a kind of pent-up stream of garbage-thoughts, cruelties and deviances. It fills you, in the secret places, in the fat deposits between the layers of your skin. You become composed of this repressed filth, indistinguishable from it. You are walking it, sweating through it. Remember, as you read the book, all the worse images that live in you, that you cling onto and helplessly reproduce. Make each horrible image that much more unbearable. Make each hyper-violent episode that much more perverse. Fill the Beryl, I mean, or Beryl means. We mean. Don't forget to do it.

Blood Type[21]

A study conducted in Korea found that women with Type B blood could have more wrinkles. Did Elizabeth Báthory have Type B blood? We may never know. Nicole Tallman is, however, certain that Julie/Sylvia has Type O Negative blood. Very goth indeed.

Bonkers (see Wild Third Voice)

Dr. Dumb

Dr. Dumb is a real doctor, at least in this book, and his real name is Dr. Plum, not to be confused with Professor Plum from the board game Clue. He's not all that dumb, but he has two messages for you, if you'll listen—one that he transmitted while living, and one while dead, and he's not sure which is which now:

I have tried to heal Julie, but I am out of treatment options. She will probably be committed here forever.

I killed Hannibal's dog, Ted. I have no remorse. An eye for an eye for what he did to my most precious pet, Violet.

Elizabeth (Erzsébet) Báthory

Hungarian countess Elizabeth (Erzsébet) Báthory may have tortured and murdered hundreds of young women in the early 16th and 17th centuries. She may

---

[21] Not to be confused with typing in blood, which would be gross and not work so well. That said, we are planning a special edition of the book printed with blood in place of ink. That blood is drawn from the authors and so it is a quite limited edition. You should not try to acquire it. You can't afford it. Inquiries about the blood-set edition auction are to be directed to Josh Dale, editor, Thirty West.

have also bathed in the blood of virgins in an attempt to recapture her lost youth, but the evidence is not conclusive. She holds the Guinness World Record for the most prolific female serial killer.[22]

Exorcism

According to a 2022 article written by Danae King in *The Columbus Dispatch* (the 11th result that came up in a Google search on "exorcism"), there are about 150 Catholic priests in the U.S. who practice exorcism, and there is a protocol for performing the exorcisms that is mentioned on the United States Conference of Catholic Bishops' (USCCB) website, though no direct link is provided. This protocol, according to Wikipedia now, is outlined in an 84-page document called *Exorcisms and Related Supplications* and is a translation of the Latin *De Exorcismis et*

---

[22] This, of course, assumes that you don't consider rich people to be definitionally serial killers. If Beryl had opinions, Beryl would be of the opinion that Billionaire is a subcategory of serial killer, and quite easily the most terrifying. When you have a billion dollars that means you are choosing to just let people die for no reason at all, and for no real personal gain. So it must be that you enjoy watching the deaths you allow, enjoy the power over life and death - the power to make live or let die, as Foucault famously defined *sovereignty*, if I'm recalling correctly. I always figured Paul McCartney stole that line from an early translation of Foucault's *Society Must Be Defended.* Am I recalling the title of that essay correctly? And anyways the question is: defended from who? From the very rich, of course. From the echelons of sovereign murderers. What I mean is that, sure, Bathory gets the record book acknowledgements and all that, but she doesn't hold a candle to even a minor Walton.

Supplicationibus Quibusdam. Nicole Tallman does not have time to read it prior to her publisher's book submission deadline in two days because she has a full to-do list, but the USCCB's November 2014 newsletter (yes, Nicole is jumping around online again) states the complete print version will only be provided to bishops and exorcists of which she is neither. The newsletter also states that a set of prayers and supplications from the text to combat evil will be made available to the faithful, and this must be why she is unable to access it.

Father

Father is not a real Priest. He is an archeologist with a bad sense of direction, and he left this message in Grand's graveyard for you: *Gabriel and I have tried to exorcize Pan. We were unsuccessful. May God Bless Julie and hold a place in Heaven for her wayward soul.*

Flowers

There are more than 830 varieties of Viola (not to be confused with the string instrument and more commonly known as violets), 2,000 varieties of Lilium (not to be confused with the drug Lithium or Nicole's dead great aunt Lillian—may she rest in peace—and more commonly known as lilies), and more than 32,0000 members of the Asteraceae family (not to be confused with, oh, I don't know, the stars?), and more commonly known as daisies, which are also a member of the sunflower family, and of which the English Daisy is referred to as "bone flower," and we won't even go there. (Nicole Tallman is not a florist, a botanist, or a horticulturist.)

Fun Facts

Some may consider some of these endnotes to be fun facts. Some may consider them annoying. Some facts may not even be real facts. You can use Google, the ultimate authority, to fact check the fun "facts" yourself. This book also contains a few footnotes that fracture the main narrative. There's a case to be made for making reading more interactive by pulling the reader in and out of the story and introducing substories or competing realities. DFW (the author, not the airport or shoe store) had something like 200 pages of notes at the end of *Infinite Jest,* and some of the endnotes have footnotes and one is 30+ pages long, so don't call Beryl and Nicole (the authors of these notes) complicated or long winded! Nicole has never finished *Infinite Jest* (she wonders if Beryl has)[23] but she has finished Marcel

---

[23] Beryl is not a real person, but rather a genderless pseudonym. Beryl would like an author biography that reads *Beryl Cooper believes in the death of the author but prefers dismemberment.* No, that isn't true. Beryl is an imaginary character, not a person, so has no wants but rather speaks whatever wants are attributed to said character. The author function ventriloquizing Beryl was very much enamored of *Infinite Jest* at a certain formative life-stage, and still, as the kids once said, *stans* both that particular work and its (...) author. Though truth be told the other large messy 'postmodern' novel Beryl's ventriloquist read at about the same time was *House of Leaves* and that has had more influence on the Beryl-designated sections of this book than did DFW's tome. On the other hand, Beryl doesn't know, and Beryl's ventriloquist doesn't know either, and said (...)

Proust's *Du côté de chez Swann.* She has also lied once or twice about reading all seven volumes of *À la recherche du temps perdu.* She apologizes for other literary lies she has told to save face or while drinking.

Gabriel

Gabriel is actually a short-order cook and he left this message in the asylum kitchen for you: *Julie's exorcism was my first. I've never seen such pain, such delusion. Pan is so strong. I will continue to pray for Julie's soul.*

Grenouille, Jean-Baptiste

Nicole Tallman's second-favorite literary character of all time, the protagonist of *Perfume: The Story of a Murderer* by Patrick Süskind, and who "Grand" claims to be.

Hannibal Lecter

Thomas Harris first introduced readers to Dr. Hannibal Lecter in 1981 via the novel *Red Dragon.* This novel became part of a quadrilogy comprising *The Silence of the Lambs* (1988), *Hannibal* (1999) and *Hannibal Rising* (2006). Hannibal Lecter is Nicole Tallman's all-time favorite literary character, and she is putting this on the record here.

---

ventriloquist is being puppeteered by another, and so on and so on, an endless regression of hands plunging into backs and working the mouths of others, a cascade of thrown voices throwing thrown voices. Halls of mirrors. Tape loops.

Ibrahim Sofiyullaha

Ibrahim. That is his surname, but he prefers to go by it. It is not his father's name, nor his grandfather's. That is common in his home country, Nigeria, where some people inherit their great-grandfathers' names and share a kinship bond through them. This is different from some western parts of the world, where a child's surname is usually the fathers. He is in his final year at an engineering university, but he has a passion for writing. He comes from a humble background, with a father who is a peasant farmer and a mother who is a petty trader. He knows how important childhood is in shaping who we become. That is why his chapters explore the protagonist's early years.

Ibrahim is a nature lover and an adventurer. He likes to observe nature as it is, to gaze at the green grasses with admiration. He pays attention to the details, the small ones that others might overlook. He notices the dripping of a tiny drop of water from a large bowl, the breeze that makes him rethink life or embrace it more. With this bio, you can tell who wrote what, even without seeing the names at the top of each chapter.

He loves history. He works as a news writer for a leading digital media establishment in Nigeria. He enjoys reading poetry from other languages, such as Chinese, Korean, French, Arabic, and some Indian literature. He is fascinated by the magic of simple details that get lost in translation. He reads multiple versions of the same poem.

This work is his first printed publication. It is a dream that he has pursued for a long time. And the fact that it is happening abroad, in the highly esteemed USA, makes it even more special. It means a lot to him. A whole lot. You can reach him at sofiyullahaolaitan@gmail.com. Feel free to send him a message if you have any thoughts—good or bad.

Julie

Nicole Tallman debated whether to name Julie "Julia" because the latter sounded a bit better alongside "Sylvia," but ultimately decided it might be too cute. Also, does one letter make all that much difference? Just ask the letter "l" when writing the word "public" or the letter "o" when writing the word "county."

NAT

Nicole Tallman had contemplated a pseudonym for this book of NAT, N.A. Tallman, or N. Alicia Tallman hoping it might stick and she might be considered one of the greats, like DFW or JCO, T.S. Eliot or V.C. Andrews, or F. Scott Fitzgerald or M. Night Shyamalan. She then realized she had already created enough confusion with her @natallman social media handle and would like everyone to know that her name is indeed Nicole and not Natalie. Please respect her relative and rapidly disintegrating privacy and conflicting wishes for literary fame regardless.

Nicole Tallman

Nicole Tallman is a real person. She realizes that "Tallman" may sound like a pen name, but it is not. She is not hiding behind a man—tall or otherwise. She is also neither tall nor a man. She is a woman of average height, if 5 '5 is considered average these days. She may be rounding up half an inch. She used to wear high heels often but has reached the age where the added height isn't worth the resulting foot pain. She would very much like this book to be made into a movie. She has nothing concrete against Hollywood. (Her favorite movies are *Hannibal* and *Perfume: Story of a Murderer*, and a bunch of French movies you've probably never heard of.) As a poet, who has published thus far with small independent publishers, she imagines this movie may do best as an independent film. She would not, however, object to someone handing her a large advance and fat royalty checks subsequently so she can spend more time writing. She does not dislike her day job. She works in government and finds it funny that the government ended up in this book. She did not write the government sections of this book. She did write her sections of this book at ungodly hours. Some might call them blue. Some might call her a little blue at times. She may be a huge Sylvia Plath fan. Nicole knows she is not Sylvia Plath, but you can read her poetry on her website. It's much better than the poems in this book. At least her dad thinks so, as well as the publishers who have published her books, and the people who have bought them (she thinks). Nicole also loves perfume. Her current signature scent is The Coveted Duchess Rose by Penhaligon's. Its head note is mandarin. Its heart note is rose centifolia. Its base note is vanilla, which may sound basic, but it's not. Vanilla, when done right, is delicious, as is rose. This is not your grandmother's perfume, although maybe she is wearing it, and that means your grandmother has great taste. Nicole is a Cancer sun, Virgo moon and Taurus rising. Her Venus is also in Cancer and her Mars is in Leo and her Mercury is in Gemini. There's a lot more, but she'll leave a little to the imagination. This is the longest bio Nicole has ever written and she is putting it here because it is much too long to fit on the back cover, and she knows other content must go there. This is Nicole's fiction debut. If you like it, let her know at nicoleatallman@gmail.com. Maybe she'll write some more fiction after this.

Ouija Board

Writing poems with a Ouija board can be fun but may also be ill advised. Nicole Tallman has written a few poems with a spirit named TOO DARK and has lived to see another day, or has she? Maybe the Nicole who is writing this endnote is a ghost of the Nicole who wrote the poems with TOO DARK. Nicole was/is a ghostwriter after all. How does one credit the ghost of a ghostwriter?

Pan

Pan is the only real spirit in this book. Pan left a message for the poets who are reading this book: *Julie was so easy to possess. When you want fame enough, you'll sell your soul. Take note, Poets. I'm coming for you all.*

Perfume

Nicole Tallman thinks you can tell a lot about a person by the fragrances they wear and the scents they are drawn to. She holds in high regard, and in no particular order: Penhaligon's, Commodity, Imaginary Authors, Givenchy, Roger & Gallet, Aftelier Perfumes, Labo, Replica, Jo Malone, Makers of Wax Goods, and Diptyque. She would also like to meet Jean-Claude Ellena, Christine Nagel, and Chandler Burr. She would love to be a paid scent critic if *The New York Times* would like to give her a column. Her Top 5 Favorite Nature Scents are:

Fire in the fall

Pine trees in winter

Freshly cut summer grass

A French field of lavender

A rose bush after a rainstorm

She also loves peonies from Whole Foods and often buys extra pine-scented Christmas products from Bath & Body Works so she can use them year-round. (Don't judge.) She also loves the smell of orange and linden blossom, labdanum, vetiver, moss, some bubblegum, and most old books. She loves Campari because it smells (and tastes) like dirt, and if you want to grow her an herb garden, she is partial to rosemary, basil, oregano, and dill. She also likes the Violet Marvis and Fennel Tom's of Maine toothpaste. Don't get her started on body wash and deodorant. We'd need many more words for that.

Nicole once smelled a perfume in Paris with a ginger note that made her gasp with shock and delight. She does not remember the name of it, if she even knew. She did not like the smell of sewer in the summer streets of Paris, and pretends she prefers Aix-en-Provence. She still loves Paris.

Nicole loves the smell of gasoline but understands the hazard of gasoline-scented candles.

Nicole once smelled skunk cabbage on a field trip in elementary school and was the only child who wasn't repulsed by it. As an adult, Nicole wrote a poem about it, but never published it. You can read it if you ask her. It contains a line about the anal glands of a civet. Some people laughed when she workshopped it. She was being serious. She even left out the reference to indole. She wants to know which smells you are drawn to.

Professor

The Professor (whose real name is Sylvia) does not really have a Ph.D. or an MFA so no one inside academia really cares what she thinks, but she does have a message for whoever still gives her an ounce of credibility: *This poor ill girl [Julie] who thinks she's Sylvia Plath. Her poems are dreadful. I'm referring her to an art therapist and a good poetry class.*

Psychiatric Torture

Here is a brief list of "treatments" women have been subjected to throughout history under the "care" of doctors in asylums: bloodletting, purging, vomiting, mechanical and chemical restraints, organ removal, trephination (removal of small part of the skull), tooth extraction, lobotomy, various shock therapies, hydrotherapy (buckets of cold water poured over the head, shockingly-cold shower sprays, hours-long soaks in tubs of ice, bodies tightly wrapped in wet cloths, vaginal hot water injections) fattening, rest cure (laying in a dim or room with very restricted movement or activity), insulin coma therapy, fever therapy (injecting patients with diseases like malaria to induce fever), rotational therapy (spinning), pelvic "massages," isolation, and inhalation of foul-smelling substances. [Nicole Tallman is not a psychiatrist or a sadist, but as of November 28, 2023, which happens to be the birthday of two of her exes (Note to Cancers: Sagittarius is not a good sign for you romantically), the word "torture" appeared 12 times in this book.]

Rabbits

Note for Beryl and/or their ventriloquist from Nicole: There are 29 species of long-eared mammals belonging to the family Leporidae (not including and not to be confused with hares.) Nicole is not cuniculturist (and isn't sure that's a recognized term anyway because autocorrect is redlining it) and stole this rabbit fun fact from Encyclopedia Britannica—the online version not the print version, though she misses the print encyclopedias of her childhood as especially those lining her parents' bookshelves. She wishes she could draw all 29 species of rabbit here so Beryl could see the difference and share those differences with the narrator he has created, but Nicole fears it may all be too confusing because jackrabbits are actually hares, and rockhares are actually rabbits, and what in the hell is up with that?

Rain

In 1939-1940, it rained for 331 consecutive days. The location of the measured rainstorm was Maunawili Ranch on the island of Oahu in Hawaii.

Red Comet

The best Sylvia Plath biography Nicole Tallman has ever read is *Red Comet: The Short Life and Blazing Art of Sylvia Plath* by Dr. Heather Clark. It was a Pulitzer Prize Finalist. Dr. Clark is currently working on an Anne Sexton biography, as announced by the author on X (formerly Twitter) on October 5, 2022. Nicole is fairly confident that this biography will be the best Anne Sexton biography she will ever read as well. Nicole would love to meet Dr. Clark.

Sylvia Plath

If you don't know who Sylvia Plath is and/or don't care to, you can stop reading, although Nicole Tallman is kind of impressed you got this far in the book without Goggling and/or paying attention to the clues throughout the narrative. You will not be receiving a Good Reader Award like Nicole received from the school librarian in 4th grade. Let me guess, you never received a free one-topping Personal Pan Pizza® from Pizza Hut via the BOOK IT! program either?

Telekinesis

According to BBC Science Focus Reporter Stephen Kelly, the creators of *Stranger Things* originally based the show around human experimental programs conducted by the CIA in the 1950s with the purpose of developing mind-control techniques to give America a leg up in the Cold War. These experiments involved the use of LSD and the records have been largely destroyed.

Triplets

The chances of conceiving identical triplets naturally are unclear but appear to be about 1 in million pregnancies. The chances of having a child with some forms of albinism are 1 in 18,000-20,000 pregnancies in the U.S., which is much higher than in other parts of the world, and these chances increase when both parents carry the gene. The chances of having conjoined triplets are 1 in a million (which can't possibly be right if the chances of even having triplets at all are 1 in a million.) The chances of having triplets with albinism are at a minimum, 1 in 10 billion. The chances of having conjoined triplets with albinism are unclear. (Nicole Tallman is not a geneticist and doesn't feel like Googling any more today and is finding the answers wildly all over the place anyway.)

Weavy Asshole

Sylvia Plath referred to Assia Wevill as "Weavy Asshole." This nickname is not a Nicole Tallman invention. Sylvia also made the nasty comment about Wevill's many purported abortions. It's important to note that six years after Sylvia killed herself, Assia also killed herself (also via gas) and her four-year-old daughter with Sylvia's former husband, Ted Hughes. Ted Hughes and Sylvia Plath's daughter, Frieda Hughes, is fortunately still alive. (She once sent Nicole a private message on Instagram.) Their son Nicholas, sadly, is not.

Wild Third Voice

Is a term Nicole Tallman learned from poets Denise Duhamel and Maureen Seaton and is not elsewhere referenced in this book but is otherwise important to note because it is a voice, often extreme and hybrid, which emerges in collaborative writing. This may justify the "bonkers" descriptor the publisher (Josh Dale) gave to the book about midway through conception.

Witch Trials

Nicole Tallman had originally imagined there would be a witch trial for Julie/Sylvia in this book, but she got distracted, as she tends to go off on tangents and down rabbit holes when writing collaboratively (and sometimes when writing solo and sometimes in general, when talking to herself and others) and decided that the witch hunt in this book should be focused on collecting child witches and warlocks ages 2-12 who had committed murder with their special powers and to institutionalize them for the purposes of a more interesting narrative. Those fictional murderous children were never put on trial either because they drowned with Julie and everyone else in the flood. Nicole figures this is ok because enough witch trials have been conducted throughout history. However, Google also brings to Nicole's attention (unprompted) that modern day witch hunts of children are still occurring in parts of the world, including Tanzania, where children with albinism are associated with supernatural powers and, therefore, become targets for wealth-building and disease-curing rituals.

Worm-Bears

Worm-Bears have been mentioned at least once in this book, and they lurk throughout (behind corners, in the interstices and page breaks). They are marginal in the over-literal sense. And they are crawling around in the shadows, eating characters and those imagined but never named almost-characters that in film are called *extras* or *background actors* and in video games are called *non-playable characters* or *NPCs*. What are those called in books—the figures that go unnamed and come into focus, if at all, in the over-invested reader's mind, members of crowds, passersby, the children assumed to assemble behind the doors of a schoolhouse an actual character walks by or into?

Anyways, worm-bears are maybe worms that are the size and ferocity of bears, wooly worms with fearsome bear claws & bear teeth. Or maybe they are bears that swarm with worms, that are punctured by thousands of wriggling nightcrawlers, that are furred, even, maybe, with worms instead of hair. Or they are something else, some other sort of hybrid or mistake or something else entirely.

Zero

The number of times the authors of this book have met in person, plus the number of times the authors had spoken to each other prior to writing this book together. This book was written collaboratively in 30 days by three busy strangers in three different time zones. We gave it our all and hope you enjoyed it. With thanks to Josh Dale and the Thirty West Team for the opportunity and to all who have supported us.

PATIENT INTAKE FORM

Maudsley Hospital
Denmark Hill, London SE5 8AZ, United Kingdom
Phone 020 3228 6000
Case Number: 13666
Attending Physician: Dr. Peter Plum
Primary Physician: Dr. John Horder
Committed: Involuntarily
Ward: Women's
Patient Name in Full: Julie Lucas (via driver's license)
Last Known Address: 33 Fitzroy Road, London NW1 8TP, United Kingdom
Date of Birth: October 27, 1932
Date of Admission: February 11, 1963
Time of Admission: 11:45 a.m.
Sex: Female
Height: 5' 9
Weight: 120 pounds
Eye Color: Brown
Hair Color: Blond
Education: College
Occupation: Writer
Marital Status: Separated
Children: 2
Religion: N/A
Number of Previous Admissions: Zero
Accompanying Physical Illness: Fever, upper respiratory infection
Toxicology: Phenelzine, Codeine, Drinamyl, Phenylpropanolamine, Carbon Monoxide
Pregnancy: N
Case Notes: Patient arrived by ambulance after attempting suicide by carbon monoxide poisoning and presents as severely disoriented. Claims to be the poet Sylvia Plath and currently separated from her husband, with whom she has two children (ages 1 and 3). Further evaluation needed once the patient is stabilized.

Acknowledgments

Beryl Cooper would like to acknowledge that the pun is groan-worthy & the pseudonym thing grating.

Ibrahim Sofiyullaha is grateful to all the invaluable and largely immeasurable support of his father, who expended his energy to procure a laptop for him to kickstart his writing career. He also expresses gratitude for the immensely needed support provided by his girlfriend, Rayo, throughout countless nights spent typing away on the devices.

Nicole Tallman wishes to thank Beryl Cooper and Ibrahim Sofiyullaha for collaborating with her on this book, Josh Dale for taking a chance on #antiwrimo and this "bonkers" novel, Maryam Qureshi for her editorial magic, and Jenn Zed for the cover design.

About The Author

Beryl Cooper is not real, or rather is not 'real' insofar as that means the name is appended to a fleshy walking body. Beryl Cooper is a feint, a joke, an author-function. The 'real' Beryl Cooper would be, one imagines, charming and a bit mischievous and holding some sort of old-fashioned cocktail. The person hiding behind the Beryl Cooper mask is an obscure Californian who shares a name, though not its spelling, with a prominent criminal.

About The Author

Sofiyullaha is a budding Nigerian writer who loves to tell stories and capture the beauty and drama of nature. He has an eye for the subtle nuances that enrich his descriptions and imagery. He enjoys reading poems, history, and war stories. He is always eager to learn and grow as a scriber.

About The Author

Photo Credit: Militza Rodriguez Boada

Nicole Tallman is the author of three previous collections: *Something Kindred*, *Poems for the People*, and *FERSACE*. She lives in Miami, where serves as the official Poetry Ambassador. *Julie, or Sylvia* is her collaborative fiction debut. Find her on social media @natallman and at nicoletallman.com

About the Publisher

Follow us on:

Scan the QR code to visit

www.thirtywestph.com